The
Woman
Who
Never
Cooked

FIRST SERIES: SHORT FICTION

MARY L. TABOR

The Woman Who Never Cooked

STORIES

MID-LIST PRESS
Minneapolis

Mid-List Press publishes books of high literary merit and fresh artistic vision by new and emerging writers and by writers ignored, marginalized, or excluded from publication by commercial and mainstream publishers. Mid-List seeks to increase access to publication for new writers, to nurture the growth of emerging writers, and, generally, to increase the diversity of books, authors, and readers. Mid-List Press is a tax-exempt, 501(c)(3), not-for-profit literary organization.

Library of Congress Cataloging-in-Publication Data
Tabor, Mary L., 1946-
   The woman who never cooked : stories / Mary L. Tabor.
      p. cm.
   "First series: short fiction."
   ISBN-13: 978-0-922811-68-7 (trade paper ed. : alk. paper)
   ISBN-10: 0-922811-68-7 (trade paper ed. : alk. paper)
   I. Title.
   PS3620.A26W66 2006
   813'.6—dc22

                              2005037908

TABOR
MARY L.

Printed in the United States of America.
First printing: April 2006

Cover and interior design: Lane Stiles
Fabric design for cover: Robin Getsug Taple

Some of the stories in this collection have previously appeared, sometimes in slightly different forms, in the following: "Guarding the Pie," *Chautauqua Literary Journal;* "Madness and Folly," *River City;* "The Woman Who Never Cooked," *Image;* "To Swim?", *Mid-American Review;* "The Burglar," *Chelsea;* "Sine Die," *Hayden's Ferry Review;* "Proof," *American Literary Review;* "Losing," *Jewish Currents;* "Rugalach," *New York Jewish Week* and *Washington Jewish Week.*

The epigraph on p. 3 is from Paul Celan's poem "Pain, the Syllable," *Paul Celan: Glottal Stop, 101 Poems,* translated by Nikolai Popov and Heather McHugh (Hanover and London: Wesleyan University Press, 2000). Used by permission.

Forgotten things
grasped at things to be forgotten,
earthparts, heartparts
swam,
they sank and swam.

—Paul Celan

Contents

Acknowledgments

I offer my thanks to Michelle Herman, who had faith in my work when it did not deserve that faith and who is my friend despite her protest that she can never befriend a former student.

I offer my profound thanks to Melanie Rae Thon, whose passionate response to my work and unwavering belief in it sustained my hope, and who honors me with her friendship.

I say to Bonnie Riedinger, "Who else would reread the same story again and again and suffer the minute questions about one stubborn phrase?" And I answer, "Only she, who is both friend and poet."

I thank Marianne Nora and Lane Stiles for taking a chance on me and Mary Logue, who understood before she edited.

I remain in debt to each of the editors who have published my stories, with particular thanks to Richard Foerster and Mike Czyniejewski. A writer does not forget such editors who care so deeply for the written word and for those who sit alone with it in their attics.

For now and forever, I owe Del Persinger, my best friend, who understands and whom I thank, with T. S. Eliot's words, for "something given and taken, in a lifetime's death in love / Ardour and selflessness and self-surrender."

Proof

Timothy could hear her confusion in rustling cloth, bags, coat, the hem of her skirt. She got on with three bags: an athletic duffel on one shoulder, a briefcase hanging on the other, and a leather handbag she shifted from one hand to the other to get the fare from her pocket and then tried without success to readjust the shoulder bags that had slipped down to her elbow and bumped against the insides of the bus. She was tall, slender. Delicate, he thought, when finally she sat down that morning in February, the first time she got on the bus he took to work. Like the new maple he'd planted in the yard last spring.

When he saw her from the window at her stop, when he watched her get on the bus each morning, everything about her made him think of trees. Her hair, light brown and mussed, made him think of fallen oak leaves. Her long, slender fingers curled around the edges of the book she pulled from one of her bags reminded him of the tender, narrow branches of his mother's backyard pear tree in winter. The way she swayed in the gusty winter winds made him think of weeping willows in summer. Her arms and elbows, legs and knees mixed up with all her bags made him think of her with perching birds—little finches, gold and red, tiny blackcapped chickadees, blue-headed vireos—fluttering about her, looking for a spot to rest.

When he woke up, she came into his head the way she came into focus when the bus slowed to pick her up. While he got dressed in the morning, while he watched his wife Caroline in the kitchen packing Josh and Susan's book bags and lunch pails, chattering with them about milk money and homework, while he drank the coffee Caroline poured into his cup, he thought about the woman on the bus.

He thought about her in spite of what he ought to be thinking about—his work, of course, Wagner's defense, and Caroline. Warm, steady, solid Caroline.

"Remember, Josh has ice hockey practice tonight," Caroline said, taking his empty cup to the sink.

He didn't remember. Maybe it was on his calendar at work. But he was planning to work late tonight, get his thoughts together for the voir dire of the jury.

Josh ran past the kitchen table out the back door. Timothy reached out, mussed the cap of shining black hair sliding past him. "It's tomorrow. Right, Josh?"

Josh was out the door, Caroline calling to his back, to his sneakers racing for the school bus. "Tonight, Josh, and Daddy will be there. Now zip your jacket all the way up—" She closed the door and pulled a slim cookbook from the floor-to-ceiling shelves Timothy had built for her.

It had been hard to fit the shelves in the narrow space between the door and the refrigerator, but he was good at this kind of knotty problem, liked the chance to work with his hands while he thought about the way he'd build a legal argument. Watching her take down the pastry book, the one with the torn, batter-stained dust cover, made him wish Caroline would ask for some kitchen project he could work on while he thought about the Wagner case. But Caroline asked less and less of him these days with his schedule getting tighter, his days longer, and he never got around to telling her he'd like the work. He should do that.

"Susan, run and get the brush. We'll do a French braid." Susan disappeared, running up the stairs. And Caroline was so busy with the children, with the catering business she was building.

Building, working, scheduling. The "oughts" and "shoulds" he sorted out from his hard-earned beliefs and set regularly, eloquently, before juries seemed like a cluttered mess at home, a mess that Caroline kept ordered for him.

"And bring the narrow pink grosgrain ribbon. I'll weave it in."

"Oh, Mommy, I can't find it," Susan called from her bedroom.

"Look on your bureau. I took it out when we laid out your clothes last night, remember?"

That old oak bureau. They'd bought it at the antique store in Kensington after Susan was born. He remembered how he'd slid the empty drawers open to check the ease of the glide, look at the grain of the wood. Drawers now filled with sweaters and blouses and ribbons—and in a blur of textures he'd seen and felt, *she* came into focus, his eye on the grain in the edge of her skirt, on the weave of wool, when she sat and her heavy black coat slid away from her knees.

Susan reappeared, ribbon streaming from her hand.

He saw the silky cuff of her blouse when she reached up to drop one of her bags from her shoulder. The little bones of her wrist. How he'd like to fold his fingers around them, see how she might fit inside the circle of his hand.

"You won't forget about tonight." Caroline put the book in the canvas bag she used to carry the little paring knife for garnishes, the torch he'd shown her how to handle without burning herself so she could caramelize the tops of crèmes brûlée. She took a spatula from the copper samovar they'd found at the flea market on Wisconsin Avenue.

"No late afternoon calls, Tim. No unscheduled meetings. This is on your calendar. I called the office, made sure it got marked down."

She has everything in hand, he thought.

He had the Wagner case, but like everything else in his life it was not in hand. The death penalty case he'd taken on as public defender because, win or lose, it would break new ground. The kind of case that threw him into that gray area—that fuzzy, unclear place where he wandered about inside his head and ended up examining what he did and did not do the way he should.

He could count on Caroline to run things while he drifted off in thought. But he tried to do his part. "Susan, aren't you going to be late for the bus?" realizing as soon as he said it that Josh and the bus were both long gone.

He wondered if she'd be at her stop today. Would she be carrying all three bags? Would she walk past him for a seat? Would the smell of pine needles drift his way as she went by?

"Don't worry, I'll be there," he said. "At worst, I'll miss dinner and meet you at the rink. You can drop him off."

"Try to get home tonight?" She was braiding Susan's hair. He marveled at the way she wove the ribbon into overlapping silken triads, until the pattern was complete at the nape of their daughter's neck.

"Daddy, you know Mommy's taking me to school. The cooking demonstration. It's today."

"Tell me you won't forget hockey practice. Tim?" Caroline faced him. "I can't do it. I want you there to watch him."

Timothy put on his overcoat. When he reached for his briefcase, she put her hand on his wrist, "You watch him, right?" but she was looking down, not expecting an answer.

She knew he took care of Josh. She must know that. But she would be right to ask him if he was reliable, to confront him with all the wandering he did inside his head. She knew something was missing, that *he* was missing. That was why she questioned him. He wished she'd read his mind, catch him at his reverie, stop him, get him in hand again.

She ran her finger under the silver bracelet on his wrist. "All that crashing around and falling. He can barely skate." Now she looked up at him as if this were her question.

He put his hand on top of hers. That strong, capable hand. "I said I'd be there." Something to say, to reassure her. "I'll be there, Caroline." Why had it come out that way—with that scratchy sound of irritation he'd heard all morning in her voice?

"Yes, okay." She rubbed the hair on his wrist—as if with her touch she might soften that sound of static between them? "I'll count on it."

Counting on him. Yes, maybe she could read his mind.

Her hand slipped away. He stood there looking at the bracelet, a gift from her twelve years ago when they were lying in the grass, in the dark, on the University of Maryland golf course, his legs wrapped around her, her hips pressing down on his, her long black straight hair falling round his head, smelling of warm night air. She pulled the bracelet from her jeans, said it was an African rope, that primitives—that was the word she used, as if she'd researched and rehearsed her little presentation speech—that primitives running naked in the bush wore hemp tied like this around their wrists as good luck charms for the hunt. She sat on top of him, leaned her head back. Her hair fell away from her face, flushed with sex, and she told him why he could wear a bracelet. "Because your wrist is thick." He looked into her dark eyes, thought of Africa and rain forests, heavy wide green leaves, lush with morning dew, the smell of orchids or an exotic flower he couldn't name, and asked her to marry him. Now he touched the silver bracelet they'd agreed was better than a wedding band and remembered how she used to make him feel.

He walked to the bus stop trying to recall why Susan was going to school late. But all he could hear was Caroline's voice like sharp static in his head, reminding him of things he kept forgetting. Had he told her that with all the equipment, knee pads, shoulder pads, heavy gloves, waterproof pants, with so much clothing, Josh and all the other eight-year-olds could barely walk? And that when they fell, they formed a heap of helmets with mouth guards, arms, and legs, that they moved so slowly on the ice, that even though they mostly fell, he was sure that Josh would not get hurt? He should have told her that, but he knew that probably he had not.

On the bus Timothy opened his briefcase. He must get his mind on the case. He pulled out his notes. He was defending sixty-five-year-old James Wagner, accused of hiring a professional from Detroit to come to D. C. to kill his wife, sixty-eight and seriously disabled from a stroke that left her paralyzed, unable to speak. Wagner had been given up to the police by the contract killer and, in Timothy's mind, would undoubtedly be found guilty. The issue was the sentence: life imprisonment or death. Was Wagner's life worth saving? The question he must answer.

But, instead, he looked out the window, waiting for that moment when he'd see her thin, wispy shape like one of Monet's poplars. He had the transcript of his interview with Wagner's grown daughter in his hand. He reread her words about her father, "He killed my family." Then he felt the motion of the bus slow, looked up, and saw her softly blurred shape move into focus.

She got on the bus. The seat next to him was free. He thought she might take it. Her three bags tumbled to the floor. She sighed, dropped into the seat across the aisle, dragging two of the bags with her by their straps, arranging them by her feet. Her purse lay in the aisle. He slid over from his seat by the window and reached for it just as she did. He looked in her eyes—blue with flecks of white and yellow, reminding him of a Key West sky at sunset, sapphire blue and sunstruck clouds.

She said, "Oh, thanks," when he handed her the tidy black purse. The leather felt soft, fine. "I'm such a klutz," she said. He smiled, brought his hand to his face, smoothed his beard, touched his lips for a moment, a nervous gesture. He couldn't speak. He felt uprooted, confused by the sound of her voice, surprisingly young, almost the voice of a child, though he could see by the tiny lines around her eyes that she was past thirty. When he sat down again, he saw a word in the title of the book she pulled from one of her bags. *Bird*. He was sure of it. She readjusted her coat around her, and it seemed to fill with air, hiding her thinness, reminding him of the mourning dove on the branch, puffing up her feathers against the cold outside the window while he drank his coffee. She couldn't possibly be interested in birds, be reading a bird book. The thought was ridiculous, but the coincidence—the word beside her narrow hand— seemed fortuitous, irresistible.

That night when he got off the subway, walked to the bus stop, she was there, her three bags at her feet, her heavy black coat blowing round her, her arms tight against her chest, her hands bare. She leaned her head toward her shoulder, turned to look at him, a glance of blue. Again he thought of Key West water and sky, of long streaks of clouds pulled around the edges of the earth. The Keys where he'd gone years ago, alone, after law school, where he'd taken a kayak out to the shallows around the mangroves and drifted.

He smiled. She didn't look away.

"You're late tonight," he said,

Still, she looked at him. "Late?"

"I never see you on this end of the ride."

She said, "Oh, the number five bus—" as if she thought of him that way.

To keep the conversation going on the bus, he said "I usually work long hours. You?" And when he sat down next to her, she said, "Me, who me?" diverting his question. Before she got off she leaned down by his knees to gather all her bags and the scent of her, sweet, like ripe peaches or pears, drifted by him. He said, "And what do they call 'who me'?"

She stood up. "Eliot, like a guy. It's important to be one of the guys up there on the Hill," smiling over her shoulder, those delicate fingers looped around the strap of her duffel bag.

"Okay," Caroline said, "your dinner is in the oven. Josh is upstairs getting the stuff. You sure it's enough?"

The air in the house was warm and yeasty. Caroline was wearing the faded blue apron, her face smudged with flour, her long black hair pulled back in a ponytail. He could see the curve of tiny lines near her eyes, her mouth, all her smiles, their laughter, like memories on her skin. He asked himself, remembering the bus ride home, the flirty chatter: *What have I been thinking?*

He opened his briefcase, held up the folder like a shield between him and his reverie. "The Wagner case. You know, the guy I'm defending."

Caroline looked up from the mass of dough she was kneading. "So how's it going?"

"I figure it's all going to be decided in the voir dire. If I ask the prospective jurors the right questions, it could be like a can opener to their brains, work on them later after they've heard the case."

She leaned into the dough while she looked in his eyes.

He poked his finger in the soft floury ball. "What's it going to be?" and their fingers met in the rhythmic wave of her kneading.

"French bread." She smiled. "It's coming. I can feel it."

He knew what she meant, why she smiled. She often talked of the dough coming alive in her hands. And he wanted the smell of her, of bread and flour and home. He stepped toward her. "Remember when we used to argue about it? Prison or death?"

She took the pile of dough, lifted it above her head and slammed it into the wooden board. A burst of flour hit the air and the front of his suit. "I remember a lot of stuff."

"Like what?"

"When we used to do things." She stopped kneading, looked up at him again, still leaning on the board, her head at the angle of a question. "The Champagne Room—" And her voice seemed to float up from the board like the aroma of the dough that had met him at the door.

He remembered it. The restaurant in One Washington Circle where they'd had brunch that Sunday long ago. How she'd laughed about the name. "Champagne Room. Bubble, bubble, boil and trouble," she said, one month after Susan's birth, their "first date," as she called it. He ordered her a mimosa, whispered in her ear, "They have rooms here." She laughed, said, "Promises, promises," and reached up, stroked his mustache, the part that turned a reddish blonde as it grew long into his well-trimmed beard.

He watched her waiting for him to remember. And he said out loud, "Promises, promises."

"Yeah, well I'm glad you're here." She looked at him, waiting for more? Or was she thinking, that's his problem? He turned away.

"No way I could take him tonight," she said.

And there she was again—safe, back to the tasks at hand.

"The best news," she said. "I've got a big party for the week-end. The works. Full course dinner. Liqueurs and pastries. I'm doing marinated leg of lamb. I might even make money this time. Practice starts at seven-thirty. And take Susan with you, please. I really have to finish the bread." She looked up from the board. "Oh, sorry about the flour. Shouldn't you change?"

A straightforward question that he heard in terms of the "oughts" and "shoulds" inside his head—and the way they used to be together—in the hotel room with her sitting naked on top of him, arguing, "What about 'Thou shalt not kill'?" He'd said, "Even the Bible smites men down, over and over again. Death is sometimes the way, has to be." Not to be persuaded, she'd said, "And what about mercy, what about standing in the other guy's life, his whole life?" He'd kissed her hard, leaned back to look at her and said, "Okay, okay, now lay that certainty on me."

She reached into the large cardboard box covered with plastic. He'd made it for her, following her directions. A proof box, where she let the loaves rise at room temperature. The air inside the box and plastic bag that covered it warmed with the gases from the yeast and flour. Beautiful long, soft, spongy loaves, perfectly risen, came out of this box after hours of waiting, of proofing—proving they were right.

Her arms reappeared from inside the box with a long stainless steel sheet framing two loaves of French bread. She placed the sheet on the butcher block in the center of the kitchen where the yellow-handled lame with its extra-sharp blade lay beside the metal scraper she used to clean the board and the soft brush she used to whisk away unwanted flour. She'd bought the lame in Les Halles. They'd been wearing backpacks, her hair in that same ponytail, her face smudged with dirt and sweat. They saw copper pots in the window alongside a mass of tools and gadgets. She explained their names and uses to him, why she needed everything in the window. He remembered wiping her face with the blue and white cotton bandanna he'd tied around his forehead. He remembered holding her backpack while she went in to buy the lame, the only thing they could afford.

Now she slashed the loaves with the lame and transferred them with her large metal peel to the flat red bricks that lined the oven shelves. "Tim, is something wrong?" He'd been standing there, watching her. Steam hissed from the oven when she threw ice cubes into the bottom. "Tim?"

Something was wrong, but how to explain? What would he tell her? That, well, there's this woman on the bus. He felt confused, ashamed.

Her hand was on the handle of the closed oven door, her square fingers covered with dried flour and dough. Her apron, dusty white on blue. He thought of flour and water and yeast, boards and tiles and bowls, the names of esoteric tools that filled their kitchen and that he'd helped her make or buy. He thought of grosgrain ribbons and zippers and toys, and stepped toward her.

"Oh, Tim," she leaned her head on his flour-covered suit. "We're just a mess, aren't we?"

And when he said, "Yeah, flour everywhere," not addressing what she might have meant, what he thought she meant by the way her words came slow against his chest, she moved away and called upstairs, "Josh, Susan, time to go."

In the car, Susan said, "I'm working on will power."

"Sounds good." Timothy said. "Will power is good. But why now?"

"Next year I go to junior high. That means I'll be grown-up in a way, right?"

"No way," said Josh. "Last week you thought you had boobs."

"Breasts," Timothy corrected.

"Right," said Josh, "sixth-grade breasts."

"I won't be riding the bus with you next year. I get to walk to junior high, big shot."

"Let's get back to will power," Timothy said. "So why is it you need to work on will power?"

"Today at the cooking demonstration—"

"Oh, right," mumbled Timothy to himself, "late to school,

with Mom," saying it out loud, clearing through, like tuning out the static in his head.

"Yeah, well, we made crêpes for the whole class. Mom had this little portable burner and her special pan. You know the one we're never allowed to touch because it's only for crêpes?"

It was copper, like the others Caroline had bought one at a time over the years—Caroline's pans, their scratches and sheen and the smell of her kitchen. "I know the one."

"Well, Mom gave me a chance to make the crêpes at the end of the demonstration. I thought I was going to just die, and she whispered in my ear right before I started to roll the batter across the pan, the way she does. You know that way she does it, Daddy?"

He could see Caroline twirling the pale yellow batter across the surface of the pan, turning out one perfect crêpe after another, sheets of waxed paper already cut in squares ready to lie between each one.

"We had leftover ones," said Josh, "with sugar and some sweet liquor stuff for dessert tonight."

The thought of Caroline's strong capable hand swirling the batter so thin it barely covered the pan made him uncomfortable, reminded him of the things he ought to be thinking about, doing, made him long for those languorous days in the Keys, before he was married, when he drank beer in the middle of the day in the sun on the deckbar at Louie's Backyard and then rode his bike to Smather's beach. Once, he'd parked near the pier and walked along White Street, still feeling that soft tingle he got in his lips from not enough food and that third or fourth beer he should have refused. He'd found the park with all the trees and flowers marked, paid a dollar, been given a wrinkled chart that had to be returned. The orchid, bauhinia-something in Latin, leaning toward the sun away from a brick wall, hanging on a vinelike branch, a purple-pink-fuchsia blossom like the palm of a delicate hand, like *her* hand.

"Daddy, listen," said Susan. "So I had the pan in my hand and she whispered in my ear, 'Will power, will power.'"

"And?" But he was half-listening now, sundrunk on heated skies with streaks of plum and peach, and the scent of her when she leaned down on the number five bus to get her bags.

"The first one was perfect, but the second one got all stuck and gooky and Mommy had to scrape it out and explain everything you have to do when this happens. She said it was a good thing I did one right and one wrong, that she would've done one wrong on purpose if I hadn't messed up. But I don't think so. I think I could've done it if I'd held the pan just right the way she told me. So now I'm working on will power."

At the rink, Timothy bought Susan popcorn and helped Josh put on his gear. He held out the soft plastic mouth guard. "Okay, open wide. This ends talking for you. You ready?" Josh laughed and opened his mouth. Timothy inserted the mouth guard, helped Josh turn around toward the ice, patted him on the rear, and lifted him up under the arms so Josh wouldn't have to step over the small wood strip at the edge of the rink. Last week Josh had taken a tumble on that first step and had had to hold back tears. He set Josh down on the ice, leaned down and kissed the top of his helmet. "Want a little shove so you look like a champ coming out?"

Josh nodded and, hockey stick in hand, legs apart, slid forward on the force of Timothy's push.

Susan and Timothy moved to a bench to watch the practice. "And then I went for my glee club audition."

"How did that go?"

"I can sing do, re, mi with the piano, but then Miss Wilson stopped and said sing it without the piano."

"And what did she say after that?"

"She said I have beautiful eyes."

He smiled, understanding that Susan was reporting, not sure what to make of Miss Wilson's compliment, its gentle obfuscation. "Indeed, you do." Your mother's eyes, he thought and put his arm around her. "You know, when you sing in your room, when you think no one's listening, I can tell you're happy."

Susan held one single piece of popcorn in front of her mouth. "I'm not going to eat it till Josh falls down."

"Oh, do tell me why."

As Josh fell in a tumble on top of four other eight-year olds, Susan said, "Will power."

When he lay in bed that night, he thought about her name, Eliot, unusual, perfect. Then with sleep closing in, he tried to focus on the Wagner case, what the jurors needed to be thinking about. And the question he had to plant before the testimony began— Is there any case where life imprisonment without parole is not severe enough? The voir dire was the key. But how to do it?

He fell asleep with Caroline at his side and woke in cool sheets, dreaming of early morning snow, sun low in the sky, reflected on the pale olive breast of a female cardinal sitting on the angled elbow of the bare limb of a pear tree, prickly from the stripping of the cold, clouds sliding in unseen wind. He felt a stillness in his chest and thought he heard someone say, *Wasn't that a cardinal that flew between us?* But Caroline lay deep in sleep curled around her pillow.

That morning at the office he ran his finger down the list of names in his congressional directory looking for the first name "Eliot." He'd play a little game. Why not? He found one, right off, in Senator Abraham's office. "Is Ms. Brown in?" "Mr. Brown?" the voice at the other end said. But how many "Eliots" could there be? He scanned the directory, feeling out of control, like dreaming, like drifting in the kayak. He'd found three more men when he looked at his clock and realized he'd wasted twenty minutes on the game: a charge against his conscience. He felt the way the sandpiper at the beach looked to him, both ridiculous and sure, its head bobbing up and down, rooting in an old cement seawall for crumbs or insects. But he continued.

"Is Ms. Goldman in?" he said. And when the staffer for Senator Moynihan said, "Ms. Goldman's extension is busy," he scribbled down Moynihan's office number from his directory and went to the flower shop on the corner of Connecticut and L.

"You need something special," he heard behind his head. He turned to look into the hazel eyes of a woman with startling white hair, cut short, wispy round her face.

"Yes." He waited while she opened the glass doors and surprised him by stepping inside the case. She was small and light and could fit easily inside. She was wearing simple white Keds. She saw him look at her feet.

"That's me. The little old lady in tennis shoes. Now let me see what we can find."

He pointed to the flowering branches behind her. "What are they?"

"Weeping cherry." She stepped out with the long curved branches in her hands. "I cut them in late winter, did it last week—from the tree in my yard. I force them in warm water here in the shop. You want this sent? Three or four branches should do it. Boxed or in a vase?"

"A box, I think."

She laid a long narrow box on the counter. While she wrapped them, she talked. "A box is something to be opened. Blossoms and branches lying in tissue paper like a wish." She pulled a tissue from her sleeve to wipe some water from her hand before she touched the filmy white paper. Such an old-fashioned, odd little habit. His mother always had a tissue in her sleeve. He could count on it when he was little, when his nose ran. "I got a bouquet of these down in Memphis when I was just a girl. Fella cut them down in early spring, tied them with a piece of string, laid them at my doorstep." He felt as if he'd walked into a dream, with a southern accent. What was she doing in downtown D.C.? She kept talking, and he kept remembering things like snapshots tossed onto his foolishness. "You'll want ribbon, I suppose, but I could use this ropy string. Give it a special touch?" He nodded, and she cut the string with a quick snap of the scissors. A sound that took him back to when his mother would snap a loose thread from the cuff of his pants with her teeth. "He played the organ at the movie house, right up there on the stage. Before the picture started moving, Bogie and Bergman perfectly still, black and white, bigger than life, with him, a tiny miniature. I could see his shadow on the screen. He played that organ—sweet as soda pop. Played at church too. Those long fingers on the keys, hands a bit like yours. His card said, 'A case of do or die.' Can you believe that?"

Her voice, her chatter, her story, the air in the shop scented with all the gardens he'd known, made him think of his mother sitting with him under the pear tree and of the story she told him when he was little about a beautiful perfect couple that lived in a farmhouse with fields of colored grass. He remembered the quiet in her voice when she said, *They only exist when you think about them.* But he couldn't remember his mother's face. He could see the pictures on the bureaus in his bedroom, the silver frames Caroline polished with a special cloth, the faded photograph of his mother when she was young, in profile, her hair black and wavy, the gold chain, the mourning locket with her mother's hair sealed inside. She'd died three years ago and he couldn't picture her. He kept seeing her pear tree. He wondered if it still stood at the old house that had been sold. It made him think of the new maple in his backyard, the one he'd bought to replace the big one they'd lost, dead two years before he took it down, uprooted it—its roots a maze beneath the ground, a foundation he couldn't pull out. He'd finally given up, cut the roots off, covered over the hole he'd dug with earth and sod. He'd had to place the new maple where the earth was clean of roots and had been saddened that the little sapling couldn't grow in the old maple's place.

"Church and movies, organ pipes," said the woman. He watched her folding tissue over the flowers he was going to send to the woman on the bus. "And the feel of this branch in my hand." She put the lid on the box. He wanted to get out of the store so he could breathe. A case of do or die. No, I *don't* believe it. This old woman with her story made him feel foolish and just like her, dreaming and wishing, drifting and floating on shallow water. "Now you'll be wanting a plain white card," as if she had any idea what he wanted. But, of course, that *was* what he needed. He thought of mangrove trees in Florida's shallows, of roots that grow up toward the sky in search of air, and wrote, "For Eliot, who defies logic. From the guy on the number five bus."

They met for lunch at La Brazzerie on Capitol Hill, sat upstairs in a corner near the window with their hands on their laps under the tablecloth, a clean band of white space between them. Neither ordered a drink. Timothy considered a bottle of wine, how it would ease him through the lunch. When he looked over the list, Eliot said, "I have to go back to work."

"Well, then, just a glass."

Sipping the wine she said, "I have a feeling I should keep my wits about me."

"Oh, I'm safe," knowing that he wasn't, that the least he could do was tell her he was married. But he was seduced by the danger of the lunch, the chance that she'd want him, maybe already did.

And when she said, "You look dangerous to me," he knew she did.

"Me, who me?" he said, reminding her of their little bit of history.

Eliot had agreed to the lunch after a lengthy phone interview. That's how Timothy thought of it, though she asked few of the questions he'd expected when he called to see if she'd gotten the flowers. She didn't ask if he was married. She didn't ask what he did for a living. She didn't ask where he lived. She asked why he chose the weeping cherry. She knew what they were. She asked how he found her. He explained about the congressional directory. He said something about a dark-eyed junco with its tiny pink beak, something about his mother's pear tree. He couldn't remember exactly what he'd said. Instead he remembered exactly how he felt while he listened to her voice, how when he paused, she didn't fill the silence. She waited. How the empty phone air seemed to give her substance.

He closed his menu. "And how safe are you with all those bags bumping around?" When she had gotten on the bus that morning, she nearly fell on the steps, more confused and clumsy than usual. He started to get up from his seat when a man closer to the door came to her aid. She told the man she was working on consolidating her bags but couldn't decide how to do it. The man laughed and she sat next to him. When everyone got off and walked to the subway, Timothy didn't move to her side. He wanted to look at her from a distance. On the platform he leaned against a pole, ran his hand along his beard, leaned his head toward her, a nod. Her duffel bag slipped off her shoulder onto the platform. She left it there. She looked straight in his eyes. He adjusted the collar of his tweed sport coat, slipped both his hands into the pockets of his jeans and wondered if she thought him oddly dressed, perhaps unsavory. He'd worn the jeans because he wanted to look lean, a bit bohemian, not like every other pin-striped guy. He became concerned she might not show up for lunch, if she'd wonder why he didn't talk to her on the platform. But when the train came and she leaned down to get her bag, she smiled beneath the hair that fell across her cheek.

Eliot put her napkin on her lap. "I have a purse with my wallet and my keys, my lipstick. I need that for business lunches." She held up the purse. "Oh, and sometimes I drop it, for effect, of course."

He wanted to tell her how gracefully clumsy she was.

"I need the duffel bag for my tennis shoes or my street shoes, whichever pair I'm not wearing, and for my exercise clothes, my hairdryer. I need my briefcase for my comic books and lunch. What do you carry in your briefcase?"

"Questions of life and death," he said.

"Ah, so you're a hit man." She handed her menu to the waiter.

"Well, not exactly," going along with the joke but wanting to tell her what he did, tell her about the Wagner case, that he only wore jeans to the office on days he didn't need to meet clients. "Actually, I'm a very serious guy."

"I believe you're serious," she said. "So am I."

The waiter balanced large white plates on the length of his arms, bending carefully at the knees to keep his back straight. "He looks like a tightrope walker," Timothy said. And then, "Maybe you're the one who's really dangerous."

"I could be, I suppose." The waiter placed their plates before them. "But I like to work with a net when I'm on the wire."

She looked straight into his eyes, that way she had of looking at him. He melted with that gaze and said, "The wire or the net? That's the question, isn't it?"

And still she looked. He put his fork down on his plate, his hands flat on the table. He leaned forward and almost said, Your eyes are like a winter sky. She looked into her plate as his attention, his gaze, colored her skin. He thought her skin was clear as light. He thought of clouds that filled the sky like a scrim across the sun and knew he'd gone too far.

"That's how I feel about my case." Something to say, anything to recover from that look. "The Wagner case. Maybe you've read about it in the *Post?*"

She stirred the green beans on her plate. "The death penalty case, sure. Tricky stuff." And then looked up at him again. "You for it or against it? The death penalty, I mean." He let himself look at her straight on, right into those soft, sweet, questioning eyes. "I'm all mixed up about it," she said.

He remembered Caroline in the hotel room, logically arguing the merits of prison or death while she was naked, vulnerable, totally his.

"And you're the kind of juror I want."

She smiled. "And how do you plan to get me?"

"Catch you, you mean. Like that nice, safe net?"

"Well, we don't want to play it too safe, now do we?"

He was feeling light in the head, not from the wine, but from her words and then her stillness while she waited for his answer. "No, we don't." But her stillness made him think of the mourning dove in the corner of the pine's two branches, silent, still, as if awaiting death? And sobered with that thought, he said, "That's what's wrong with the death penalty. No margin for error."

"Well, that's obvious," she said, a little disappointed, sobered now herself perhaps because he'd stopped seducing her, hadn't he?

He was getting control, focusing on his business, his case. His or Wagner's? He thought, No margin for error is the point and said, "Did you know that one shooter on a firing squad always had a blank in his gun? Did you know that? Do you know why?"

She put down her fork. "Let me think about that." She ran her fingers along the stem of her wine glass. "I should think about that."

At the corner of Massachusetts and Third, she ran her finger underneath the bracelet on his wrist. He wanted to kiss her, could have. He could have wrapped his fingers round her wrist, but he didn't. He stood there, waiting. If she'd lean toward him, would he? "The firing squad and the blank?" she said as her finger slipped away. "What if they were wrong? Well, is that margin for error? I don't think so," and she crossed the street.

That night he dreamed he was floating on a raft, drifting from shore. The familiar shapes of houses and people appeared on the water, drifted in and out of focus until he was engulfed by the shadow of the clouds on the unfamiliar sea. He woke in the dark next to Caroline. She was lying on her back asleep, vulnerable and warm. He touched the soft curve of her stomach and she rolled towards him. He ran his hand along her cheek, down her neck and, half asleep, she sighed and kissed him on the mouth. He remembered once when they'd made love and she'd seemed to disappear, to have gone away instead of toward him. He'd brought her back by asking, "Where are you?" She'd said to his dismay, "Another world." And he began to pull away when she added, "I can only go away like that with you." "What do you mean?" he asked. She rolled on top of him, propped her elbows round his head. "I'm not afraid of what you'll do while I'm away."

The next morning he didn't take the bus. He needed to think about what he was doing. Why? He needed to keep his mind on his case. He told Caroline he needed the car, that he had to drive out of the city to do some research. He didn't call Eliot.

In his office he worked on the questions for the voir dire. He filled one yellow pad after another. He thought, She's all mixed up about the death penalty. He scribbled questions on his pad. The standard question of the prosecution: Are you opposed to the death penalty? He could never hope to get those jurors. They were the first to go. How to get the Eliots? He thought of a jury of slender, delicate trees, of birds seeking shelter in their limbs, building nests. He thought of kitchens and crêpes and popcorn, and pushed all the yellow pads off his desk.

He walked to the Senate office building, sat on a bench, looked at the place where Eliot worked. I don't know what books she reads, he thought. I should have asked her.

That night in bed he said to Caroline, "The other night you said, 'I remember lots of stuff.'"

She curled on her side to go to sleep. "It's late." But she turned toward him.

He brushed her hair behind her ear. "I remember lots of stuff, too." He ran his finger along the tiny cartilage, the edges and the swirls. All the little bones inside, the nerves and passages, the membrane that heard a child cry before he woke. That tiny ear that when she couldn't sleep she laid upon his chest to listen to his heart.

"And what do we do with all that stuff?"

He said, "I don't know, but we've got it, you and me, we've both got it."

"Come here," she said and then when he'd laid his head against her heart, "Yeah, we do, don't we?"

"It's time we bought a second car, don't you think? Then I can shorten my commute, stop taking the bus."

Again she said, "Come here." He wrapped himself around her, circled her inside his hold and said, "All that stuff? It's like a big wide net."

She began to cry. "But what's it for?" He knew that she was in that place deep down inside her where he'd hurt her, where he'd been missing far too long, that place that had nothing to do with the tasks at hand, that place where she was no longer safe.

He kissed her on the mouth and with his elbows propped around her head, he said, "You count on it."

He began to take an earlier bus. As the bus sped by Eliot's stop, he still hoped she'd appear, magically, like dogwood blossoms in spring floating in midair, but he felt safe when she did not.

In the voir dire, to the horror of the prosecuting attorneys, he struck for cause thirty-seven jurors who appeared unreasonably biased in favor of capital punishment. He did it with the simple question: *Is there any case so awful you could consider only death?* In the minds of those who remained, he had planted the seed that mitigating circumstances should be considered, must be considered—because, as he told them, "There's no margin for error." He had uncertain jurors, the ones who knew you could not kill without killing both the dark and the light that made a human soul.

He was sitting in his office late one night going over the case— the fact that Wagner had never before committed a crime, his years of service with his company, his education, his skills, the good he would do in prison. He was writing his summation, how he would remind the jurors of their solemn promise to consider mitigating circumstances. This murder, he would remind them, was not the worst of the worst. It made him think of Wagner's daughter, how she was right that her father had killed her family. That was the right way to put it. Not 'He killed my mother,' the accurate way to put it. Wagner had killed the whole, the light and the dark, and now these jurors, these uncertain jurors, would see that he should still be saved.

Everyone in the office was gone when the phone rang. He picked it up with the "oughts" and "shoulds" of the case merging into his own life—the way his mother's pear tree had made him think of the maple sapling he'd planted in the yard last spring.

In the moment of quiet hesitation that preceded her speaking, he knew somehow it was Eliot. She said, "I thought I dreamed you." He thought of all the little birds that fly away before you see the colors in their feathers, of all the trees he'd ever known stripped bare of leaves and bark, of the decay inside of trees after lightning split them open, cut them down to lie on dark, moist ground deep inside the forest where no one has cleared the way.

Sine Die

I see the two women at the bar, yellow silk, split skirts, dark hair, beautiful long thin legs.

The two women were at the bar, pretending they were in Hong Kong. (Much of what they do is pretending—it is how they get on with one another.) Today they pretended that they were Asian, that their hair was long and straight, that they could smoke without harm, that they could drink and stay in control but still get high, that their skin was the beautiful mellow beige of Asian women, that they could lie in the sun without burning. They talked and laughed. They wore their hair pulled back against their heads, made smooth with gel so they had the look of straight hair. They went shopping and bought yellow silk blouses and skirts, went to a seamstress who cut the slits in their skirts, who tightened the silk against their hips.

The only way to tell them apart is the younger sister's small bones, tiny points, exposed; the older's small round stomach. They bought high-heeled shoes and wore them even though both had inherited their mother's feet—one with the hammer toe, both with the bone that widened at the ball, that had become a bunion as they grew older. One sister's bunion was worse than the other's. The bunions, hidden in the narrow vamps of their shoes, hurt. They did not care. They were pretending and they were good at it.

It had taken them a long time to learn. It began when they were children, when they pretended they could fly by riding on each other's feet, when they pretended they were fine cooks like their mother, cooked mushrooms on toast and created a delightful meal for themselves without their mother's help, when their parents were not home, when the older sister was baby-sitting the younger. It was when they were children—like other children—that the pretending became an integral part of their play. But unlike other children, the pretending became so essential to their relationship that they could not, would not, outgrow it because, while they were children, one of them got sick. They didn't talk about the sickness; they pretended, the way their parents pretended, that it did not exist, but the sickness was the source of all their pretending now, the unspoken source.

The two sisters left the bar and went down Baltimore street, the street where the strippers worked the bars. They didn't go into any of these bars, but they liked to walk down the street. So they walked, watched the eyes of the men on them, knowing this was dangerous. But the older sister was strong, a powerful, sick, fearless woman who told the younger sister not to be afraid. She said, "Pretend you belong, that you own the street. Anyone can go anywhere if she acts like she owns the place."

1

This way of walking, of turning a street corner, of entering a room, is something you can learn by pretending. It's the key to everything. That's why we do it when we're little—so we can learn.

I am not sure when I am pretending and when I am not. I had a sister, three years older than I, who died. I have trouble remembering her. To help with this I think of remembering and forgetting as two sides of a right triangle. I think of the third side, the hypotenuse, as pretending. It is this third side that helps me accept the not knowing, the intangibility of the truth.

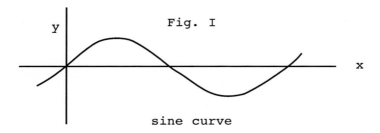

Fig. I

sine curve

In trigonometry, the graph of the equation $y = sin\ x$ is called the *sine curve*, an elegant mathematical tool for defining the relationship of the sides of a right triangle. It is an infinite (*sine die*) pattern of undulating curves with an infinite number of points that plot changes in the triangle, including a point where no triangle exists—a flat line.

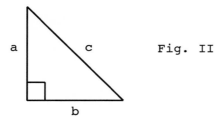

Fig. II

On the right triangle, let us call the two sisters sides A and B; A is the older sister; B, the younger; they are bound to one another in a right angle, an essential (*sine qua non*) element. Their relationship, the unknowns and knowns of each to the other, is defined by the *sine curve*. The unknowns reveal themselves as knowns, as points on the sine curve by calculating the relationships of A to B to C. Side C is the pretending. I think of the sisters (A and B) interchangeably as *remembering* and *forgetting*, for as I've said the two are hard to tell apart, the way the sisters looked alike that day on their walk down Baltimore Street.

2

The two women were not whores. They were not wild.

The only thing they had ever done together with abandon was the time they cut their long hair short and had it permed, which made their curly hair curlier—and them, ridiculous. Then, like now, they did not know exactly what they were doing, and their hair bloomed into unexpected Afros when it dried. Since puberty, each had rolled her hair and sat under dryers. Neither knew that she had naturally curly hair because both had straight hair as children. The curls came with puberty, when all those rollers became essential to their pretense of appearance. In this sense, the truth about their hair was a secret neither had known—that they discovered with a silly mistake, the permanent solution on their hair. The tameness of the mistake and the resulting discovery contrasted with the seriousness of the pretending that defined their relationship and the current adventure.

For now they both knew there *were* other secrets. Neither knew what the other had done that could have been wild, that they had not done together. Both sisters, who were married, believed that the other had never had an affair. But on Baltimore Street each sister looked at the other wondering if this were true. Had neither actually had an affair?

The older one, the one who was sick, thought, My sickness is like an affair. It seduces me to live even though I know the doctor will cut off my leg soon (this, my sister doesn't know). It repels me because I would rather die than live deformed. I am infatuated by my secret. When I am ready to tell, my horror will hold my sister near me. What has my sister kept secret? she wondered. To find out, she lied, "We tell each other everything. I would know if you had done something. I would see it in your face, hear it in your voice."

The younger knew that was not true because she had had an affair with a married man, a lawyer, many years ago, before she was married—and not told. She wondered, Would I sleep with the lawyer now? Now that I am married?

So she was not as innocent as she pretended. Did her sister know this? She was reminded of when they were both teenagers: the older had made her a costume like the yellow silk outfit she was wearing now. Her sister had called it "the gypsy costume." Now the younger saw that the gypsy costume really was the outfit of a whore, with the low-cut blouse, the skirt with a slit up the side, on a fourteen-year-old girl. The skintight skirt, which the thin little girl wore well, pretending to be older. Her thin body suited the outfit, the scarf her sister put around her forehead, a larger scarf around her shoulders atop the off-the-shoulder blouse. Who was pretending? Was it the little girl? Her seventeen-year-old sister? Both, the woman now realized. They were dreaming the shared secret, *desire*.

The sisters' most powerful secret was something each knew but would not, could not, express—the power of the older over the younger. Both were aware of it. Neither knew how it would play out.

3

My sister is dead. She died three years after our mother died. My father is sick—but because I am left I am the only one who knows about this. My father doesn't remember that my mother (his wife) and my sister (his daughter) have died. He has severe memory loss—Parkinson's disease. He is *sine cure* (without cure). The doctors simply say, to clarify, "Senility." But I think he is mad with grief. I am forty years old, married to a man I love. Like my father, I am not sure what I know. I often pretend—now that my sister and mother have died and now that my father can't remember those facts—I pretend that another man loves me, a man who has no connection to any of these losses. My husband, who I think no longer desires me, went through it all with me—all I've lost. I want to forget, to pretend. Perhaps the other man is real. Perhaps my husband desires me. My father sometimes says, out of the blue it seems—is he trying to remember or forget when he says this?—"The circumstances are extenuating."

4

Now a man approached them. Secretly the younger sister hoped they would meet an ordinary man who himself was floating down the street looking for solace while they were floating looking for danger. Secretly the older sister hoped they would meet a man looking for danger. She was dangerous because she was dying from the diabetes she'd had since she was twelve—in the '50s, after insulin had been discovered. But the disease is still *sine cure*—like the older sister's desire for danger, and her need to take the younger one along.

They walked together, laughing, the younger one feeling safe beside the older who knew what to do, how to handle herself, how to handle men, how to put them off as she did when the men who looked perverse or sick came close. She did this with a turn of her head, a swift lift of her chin, a look of disdain. It was effective, in the style of a professional hooker, and they were safe in the open street, in front of the bars where the strippers stripped. The unwanted men would turn their heads away, look in the bars, seeming to know they could not afford this whore.

But when the one in the suit, looking as if he'd come from a convention downtown, wearing the name tag he'd forgotten to take off, walked by—things began to happen.

He looked ordinary, not handsome, but clean, corporate. He was made ridiculous by the name tag he was wearing, one's name on one's sleeve, so to speak, though the tag was clipped to his right breast pocket, DONALD BELSON. The tag made him seem lost, though that was not how he looked. He looked secure, eager to explore. But the forgotten name tag made the younger sister think of one of her children on a field trip, wandering from the group, and she wanted to talk to him, the way she would to a lost child, to get him back to his group, to the other suited men who had forgotten to take off their conference ID badges. She watched him take it off when a prostitute called him by name. But she did not speak when he approached them.

5

What had he seen in them? He thought they were hookers. He was seeing the sights he'd read about in the guide book, which said to stay away from this neighborhood but that it was safe to go onto "The Block," the one section of Baltimore Street where the strip joints were, where the prostitutes wandered, but took

their Johns elsewhere. The block where Blaze Star used to per-
form at the Palace Theatre. It was worth one trip if you were
careful. He'd read about Blaze Star in the paper. Wasn't she the
one who went with that congressman? Wasn't she the one in a
movie with Paul Newman? Yes, he was saying to himself—I can
do this. I might see Blaze Star. No one will know and I'll do it.
Not everyone who comes to Baltimore Street buys a whore. And
what if I did? *Like pretending.* What would be the harm? He's a man
after all. He can take care of himself.

This was what he was thinking when the two sisters walked by.

The older sister spoke. "Where are you from?"

"Iowa. Here on a farm conference."

"You don't look like a farmer," said the younger one. Her husband was from Iowa and she was emboldened now to speak, by the
name tag, by her sister's boldness, by the calm voice of the man.

He wondered if they were fooling with him like the ones
who'd called him by name before he'd put the name tag in his
pocket, but he saw the fear in the younger sister's eyes, saw that
their clothes were pressed—and clean, like their hands, their hair.
He said, repeating himself because he was nervous, "I'm from Iowa,
a farmer, corn mainly." He stopped to see what they would do.

6

The older sister was cynical, thought the man was dangerous,
while the younger thought him safe, knowing that he was from
Iowa where streets like this did not exist.

Now we can tell the two sisters apart: Disbelief (A) and Belief
(B). This was the way the two of them could be named on the
street that day. Their relationship defined: cynic (A) and innocent (B). The farmer (C) was pretending.

7

I was no longer innocent when the doctors cut off my sister's leg: knee, shin, foot (hammer toe and bunion). I was guilty. I said to one of my nieces—the wild, drinking, crazy one, the one most like my sister, my sister's child in every way—I said, "Give me a cigarette." This doesn't sound like much. But I hadn't smoked in fifteen years. I had tried to be well.

That night I bought a pack, smoked seven in a row, fast. Binge smoked. Sat outside on my patio in a plastic white chair, drank red wine, then ruby port. Smoked seven more, went upstairs to the bathroom, sick with nicotine and booze and grief.

The next morning, the morning after the surgery to cut off her leg, while she was thrashing in her crib-bed in the intensive care unit, I called him, the married man I had slept with before I married my husband. I was sober-smoking-hungover-crazy. I called and said, "See me, anytime, anywhere." I didn't tell him what was wrong.

He said, "Sure, our old place."

"Yeah," I said, "our old place. Dark, lots of wood. We'll drink that Scotch you like?"

He said, "Four o'clock."

I said, "And I'm smoking."

He said, "Smoking what?"

"Oh, give me a break."

"Well, I was hoping." Because he smoked weed. He'd do it in public, at hockey games with his corporate lawyer friends, the ones who did criminal law, pro bono, to keep their hands in, to know the judges. He was a criminal lawyer. Had connections. He said the corporate guys brought the stuff to the games, said he never had to pay for it. And those clients in Romania—the Communist Mafia—at least that's what I'd always thought because of the way he talked about them. He'd say, "They change their offices like clothes." Like crooks.

He was dangerous.

Like my sister who was dangerous and wild—and dying.

8

They'd walked together down Baltimore Street before the city cleaned it up. They'd put on the silk yellow blouses and skirts and the high heels that hurt their feet. This was before the amputation, before the older sister's foot was cut off, the calf and knee and lower thigh, all cut off. The diabetes that killed her. Before all that.

9

I was in alien corn, like Ruth who lay at the feet of Boaz.

I wanted to lie down at the lawyer's feet. The lawyer, who drank too much Scotch, had been married too long to a woman he said he didn't love. The lawyer who said he loved me—the woman out of control, the way I—and my sister, too—had been that day we wore the yellow silk—not a good color for either of us, the color of my sister's skin when she'd lain on the gurney, life sliding away.

An emergency—when I called the lawyer. Did this man, the lawyer, love me? What could he know about love? His father was an alcoholic who'd abandoned him; his mother, a nervous woman who searched his drawers, lifted the extension when he talked with girls. And I was smoking cigarettes that, with my low body weight, made me high, gave me that out-of-control feeling I yearned for.

10

In the bar at the Hay Adams in downtown D.C., the lawyer said,
"I had the most detailed dream about you last night. A party you
organized with your husband—you, with long hair—you—and
your friends—I thought you didn't have any—and Claire." The
wife he said he no longer desired. "You and Claire sang a song
together, or maybe a poem, cheek to cheek, and almost kissed
after you finished. I never stopped holding my breath. You were
so beautiful. Such a strange dream. Not the beautiful part, but the
whole thing." I understood: he was dreaming *desire*.

I told him my dream: "A woman dreams of her niece, her sister's child, who is lost. The woman and her sister can't find her.
They know she is very smart in an odd, quirky sort of way. She
is little, barely four. And somehow someone said something to
her that confused her and caused her to go away. The woman
and her sister are searching for the child, worried she is dead. It
is very hot outside. They find her lying on a rooftop, safe and
asleep and they take her home." I saw: *abandon*.

11

The two sisters can go any place. They are *pretending*, after all.

They walked with Donald Belson past the first four strip joints,
past the bars, the noise, the men in suits with name tags, forgotten
to be removed, past the prostitutes. Can one tell who is a prostitute and who is not, for *they* were dressed like whores, weren't
they? They walked off Baltimore Street. The silliness (or was it the
seriousness?) of the game the three of them were playing could
no longer be denied. So they decided, Why not take the game to
a better neighborhood, to an upscale bar and restaurant?

Now they were not in Baltimore; they were in the Hay Adams near the White House in D.C.

"May I buy you both dinner?" the farmer asked.

"Drinks first," said the older sister.

"Yes, I'll have a Scotch," said the younger.

"You don't drink Scotch," said the older. "She'll have an apricot brandy sour."

"A Scotch for the lady," he said to the waiter and turned to the older sister, "And for you?"

"A stinger," she said. But she was off balance now. Her sister drank Scotch.

As if hearing the question in her sister's mind, the younger said, "I drank Scotch at the congressional retreat at the Greenbrier. All the men drank Scotch."

"Retreat?" he asked and then before she could answer, "Congress is a perpetual retreat from reality."

So, he was a conservative. She was a liberal, an administrative legislative aide to a senator; a high-paying job with a low-paying name, an oxymoron of sorts because it sounds like a secretary but most of these senior aides are the brains behind their senators. This fact lies unspoken. Like the power of the older sister.

She went along. "A sinecure, yes. I met a lobbyist for nuclear power there. He looked much like you, fair-haired, weathered hands. He had been the head of the plant in Ohio—a nuclear engineer with a law degree. He was about fifty at the time; I was thirty-six and I kissed him in the elevator, or rather he kissed me, but I wanted him to kiss me after three hours of knowing him."

"Did you have an affair?" said the older sister.

"If I tried to kiss you, would you let me?" the farmer asked the younger.

"Yes," and he leaned across the table, disturbing the triangle their seating had created.

Fig. III

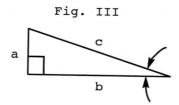

Let us call them now again side *A* for the older sister, side *B* for the younger, side *C* for the farmer. When side *A* heard about the man at the Greenbrier, she felt smaller. When sides *B* and *C* came closer, side *A* felt smaller still, in danger. She felt she was disappearing the way she would disappear when she died.

Did her sister not see this? If anyone was to have an affair, it must be she. So she stood, the right angle between her and her sister still in place but her length extended. The angle between the man and her sister widened.

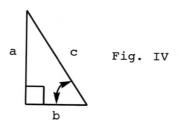

Fig. IV

"What will you do if I leave?" said the older to the younger.

But the younger was feeling brazen now. The game continues, she thought. "Sleep with him if he can afford a beautiful room here," she said and she laughed. Nothing about her was in character. She was out of control but safe because her sister was with her. She knew her sister would not allow her to do this with a man neither knew, had reason to trust. And the issue of adultery. That was there, as well. Had she committed adultery? Had she in some sense committed adultery when she kissed the nuclear engineer at the Greenbrier? She was considering this while she watched her sister consider this brazen, dangerous thing she had said.

12

So I met the lawyer at the Hay Adams and then called him the day after and said again, "Meet me." I didn't expect he would. I expected him to be busy with work, or excuses because I was not offering the expected. I was not offering myself at all. I wanted a retreat from reality. I was interested in talk and talk alone, and he knew it the way he'd always known since I had discovered he was married after I slept with him. After all, I am married; my husband loves me; I love my husband—and the lawyer knew that. But he said, "I can be on the subway in twenty minutes." Then he called back and said, "I can't wait. I'm leaving now. I'll be at the other place we used to meet. I'll be there when you come." I was alarmed. What had I done? What was he thinking? More to the point, what was I, when I said, "I'll leave now"? I drove to the familiar corner, where the subway stop is, at the Booeymonger restaurant, a joint where we used to eat oozing sandwiches with sprouts and cheese and avocado, healthy fattening like the oxymoron of our relationship: honest betrayal. Like the relationship of the two sisters. Why did he make me think about my dying sister? I was pretending she was not in the hospital, that she did not need me—the wild, all-knowing sister in her shroud. The way I was willing to see him made me think: *abandon.*

I began to count on his surreptitious phone calls when my husband was at work, before I left for the hospital to visit my sister. I began to count on hearing from him. I needed him. That's what I told myself. I was at home because I had become a political consultant after many years on the Hill, and now had found time for myself by parceling out my talents in hourly rates. I could choose not to work and often did, deciding which hours of the day I would help a particular company manage its way through the maze of committees and subcommittees considering its fate in some oddly worded legislation that would inadvertently (*sine care*) put the firm out of business, kill it.

On the day my sister died, I didn't go to the hospital.

The day before, I went with him to his apartment, to see it, to talk. This was the apartment he kept in town near his office. His family house was a farm beyond the suburbs. At the apartment, I said odd things. "Let me see your refrigerator." I noted the contents: Maille French Dijon mustard (a good brand, the one I used. Had I told him about it in passing? Had I been sharing recipes with him, told about what I had been cooking for dinner? Of course not. Was he reading my mind? Did the mustard mean we had some deep connection of taste, of desire?) Packaged ham (that looked as if it had been there awhile, had that creamy white cast to the inside of the plastic.) But I said nothing, continued noting. Unsalted butter (the kind I used to make pastry, Land O' Lakes. Why would a man living in an apartment alone have unsalted butter in sticks?— though he did have a wife on the farm where he was planting trees. He would have something in a tub, something he could smear quickly on a bagel or bread and get out. I was impressed by his butter.) The little refrigerator was crusted over with ice where the ice cube tray hung in its small metal compartment. I suggested, "Let's defrost it." He laughed, agreed; then he kissed me. I hadn't expected this. The kiss frightened me. My back did bend with my intake of breath and life and being desired, but my mouth did not give the way I had thought it would. He stepped back, apologized. Then took it back.

We had talked about the attraction between us the way two analytical people will talk most anything to death to avoid doing anything. It had been a good ploy. And he was so trustworthy in that untrustworthy way of his (having not told me about being married until after we'd slept together at the Tabard Inn). But he always answered my calls—after I married my husband. Often left his office to meet me when I needed him, and we'd agreed long ago our time was past. He ran a finger across my hand occasionally but nothing more. I had felt safe in the apartment with him, didn't think anything would happen, was sure of it. After all, he was still married, kept the apartment for convenience, near his office.

Or did he have regular affairs? I asked. He told me, No. He told me he loved me.

The next day, the day she died, I sat with my coffee and waited for him to call. He had said he was going out to the farm to plant trees, wouldn't call. I looked up at my skylight in my kitchen, saw it was raining, drops all over the plastic dome that revealed the great aged oak in my backyard. I hoped he'd gone to work, knew his calendar was clear, hoped he'd abandoned the tree-planting project. I was weakening, understanding the nature of seduction, how it worked. How the older sister had seduced the younger in the same way, by oxymoron, by withdrawn giving. He'd taken refuge and made me crazy.

13

The day the two sisters walked on Baltimore Street neither sister had understood what the other needed.

The younger had trusted the older to extract them. She believed her sister would never leave her in a difficult situation. Now she knew her sister *would* abandon her.

The older had the feeling of getting smaller in the presence of the farmer. She had had this feeling before—when the younger sister married. *She* had felt abandoned then, and never told. She wanted her sister to betray her husband. She wanted that secret to be theirs. She wanted to be present for it. What should she do now when she was getting what she wanted? She said, ignoring the farmer, "So you are a whore. The pretending is over."

The younger sister, thinking this was part of the game, said, "Yes, I'm a whore."

The farmer was confused. He did not want a whore. He wanted sex with this clean, young woman. He wanted safe sex that no one at home would ever know about. "I'm not paying for this," he said. "I'll pay for the room but nothing else."

"If he pays for the room, you're a whore," said the older sister. "I'll pay for the room."

"But that will make you my pimp," said the younger and laughed, but she was now afraid of both her sister and the farmer. "I can take care of myself," she said to her sister. "Leave. It's time for you to leave."

"And what will you do when I leave forever?" said the older one, referring to her sickness, the unspoken source of all the pretending.

The younger sister had to escape the game. She began to daydream. She dreamed that a man with the beige skin of Asians, with wire-framed glasses, with a long braid of straight black hair, a barefoot man who wore white jeans and a white shirt was on a wooden dance floor with a woman in yellow silks. They began a dance he called the labyrinth, movement they created on the floor with no speech. The man spoke only once at the beginning of the dance: "I think the rules will become obvious." And the two began to dance in front of the younger sister as if she were not there. She felt she had disappeared, that they could not see her but she could see them. The two swirled around one another touching with shoulders and heads and backs, no hands. They leaned on one another in a discord of dance, moving away and then in, without pattern, coming closer to her. Though they could not see her, she was pulled into the dance, into the triangle of movement, of the touching of bodies, her elbow on the back of the man, her sister's breast on her back. Then the three would swirl apart and the sisters would come together, leaning on each other's backs, first the younger leaning hard to bend the sister's back, then the older reversing the pressure until the man re-entered and led them in a discord of leaning and touching parts of their bodies, legs, arms, backs, buttocks, breasts, coupling and uncoupling as if pulled by the gravity of one object to another, one body part to another and in the midst of the discord, the younger sister saw the bodies connect and then part, pulled together and apart, and she saw that her sister was dying, getting smaller whenever the man in white approached. She saw that she too was dying, that she got smaller, experienced little deaths whenever either approached and she knew that she was alone, that she was the observer, who could see what her sister and the stranger could not, that the dance keeps on dancing and that discord is pattern.

Her sister said, "What's wrong with you?"

But the younger sister got up from the table, ran from the Hay Adams, from the farmer, from her sister, outside to the street. Men and women in suits, carrying briefcases, hurried by her. They walked briskly, with purpose. She was in their way. They knew where they were going, what they were doing. She was alone. Where could she go? Inside her head, she said over and over again one word: *abandon.*

14

I wanted the lawyer.

I pretended I could forget my sister who was being moved from her hospital crib-bed, who was on a gurney when her heart gave out, when they pulled off her gown, when they ran for the paddles.

And all that day, while the clouds and rain interspersed, never clearing but never falling into a full downpour either, I waited for him to call. I could not do my work, while my sister was dying, while I waited for the lawyer to call. I, a grown woman, waited like a schoolgirl by the phone for the sex-charged conversation that I thought no longer existed in my marriage. The day before, I could tell that the lawyer could not bear to be without me the way I could not bear to be without him. It was mutual, this longing that neither of us understood. But today he bore it well. I could not reach him because he was at home or he would have called. I saw the triteness and the horror (my sister) of my situation. *High-heeled shoes, hammer toe and bunion, hidden in the vamp, yellow silks, flying on each other's feet.* He was in control, wasn't he? Or was he? *If anyone was to have an affair, it must be she.* I felt foolish and depraved. But the longing for him would not go away the whole day—*So, you're a whore.*—even though I knew that if I actually slept with him, if I committed adultery, I could no longer live with myself because I loved my husband, who loved but no longer desired me. Or was it that I no longer desired him? *Bodies connect and then part. If anyone was to have an affair—If he pays for the room—I'll pay, I'll pay.* I didn't want to remember her face. I wanted the lawyer. I needed the lawyer.

How could I be so out of control and he so capable of restoring his? We had seemed alike the day before—hard to tell apart, like *the two sisters on Baltimore Street.* Like remembering and forgetting. Like sides *A* and *B* of the right triangle. Forever. Like my sister and me.

And then the call came that my sister had died.

Epilogue

On the sine curve of the right triangle, I am unable to plot the unknowns. I had thought I could do this, that I could see the two women at the bar—that I could pretend the way they did—that I could tell the story of the younger sister and the lawyer—that I would know when I was pretending and when I was not, that I could forget the way my father has. But the sine curve continues to undulate sine die. The sine qua non of my triangle is gone. Side A disappeared. Side C disappeared and I am side B, a flat line—like the flat line on my sister's heart monitor when she died on the gurney where I last saw her. Though she was naked beneath a yellow sheet, though desire had disappeared from her face, she had the arrogant look of a person who could go anywhere. My father, who stood with me by her side, said, "Out of order, out of order," over and over again.

Fig. V

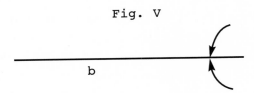

b

The Burglar

Ruth had found one silver earring lying on her bureau, opened her jewelry box, and discovered the burglary. She'd opened the top bureau drawer and saw, instead of the little white cardboard box, a faint outline of dust where the box had lain, and she was stricken with loss. The items in the box had belonged to Ruth's mother. The wedding band etched with forget-me-nots, the gold locket, the ivory cameo with the raised but barely etched body of a woman, the choker of pearls. In the burglar's hands. Ruth could no longer touch them, could not put on the gold chain with the wedding band askew, a circle off center as it hung on an angle from the chain. Lost. Another part of her mother who had died the year before. More loss. More than she could take? And then the fear. The burglar. Who was he?

Ruth and Ben, her husband, had come home from visiting their daughter at college, a train trip from Wesleyan in Connecticut. Ben had found a window jimmied open in the sunroom and called the police, who said the usual things: professional job. Be glad the house wasn't trashed. Recovery? Unlikely. We'll call you. Yes, a security system might be a deterrent. Chevy Chase is an easy hit, close to the District line and you're only one house from Connecticut Avenue, the police said—as if Ruth and

Ben should have known better when they'd bought the house. As if the burglary were their fault.

Now, when Ruth would come home, she would stand in the doorway and yell, "Anyone here?"

Recovery? Unlikely.

The policeman's words.

Now, questions in Ruth's head, whenever she took off her clothes to shower, while she studied her small breasts in the mirror and saw, instead, her mother's large, soft breasts that her mother had said she'd ruined by binding them when she was young in the 1920s, when her full-bosomed top and round bottom were anything but the flapper's desirable flat shape.

Ruth was often naked with her mother. When her mother was young, she'd be naked—to keep her clothes dry—when she'd bathe Ruth. She was an efficient, practical woman. She'd straighten the linen closet naked. She could be seen changing a light bulb naked. If something needed to be done, Ruth's mother did it. Nakedness had nothing to do with what needed doing.

The burglar, Ruth thought, was efficient, practical, neat. He'd not taken any of her costume jewelry. He'd not taken the cheap silver earring she'd found on the bureau.

One night after the burglary, while she stood naked, while she looked at her breasts that her husband and other men had touched—her breasts that none of these men had spoken of, her breasts so unlike her mother's—she wondered what she'd feel if a man, if Ben, found words. Or was this moment, while making love, this moment of body, of mind, of touch—ineffable?

"Recovery? Unlikely," she said out loud. And then, "The burglar."

The burglar, who was dissatisfied with the contents of the little white box that he'd tossed into his briefcase at the end of his search. The burglar, who touched the old items and assessed their value—less than he'd hoped—an 18-carat gold locket (in the shape of a fleur-de-lis, oddly sealed with black glue where it had been opened, something inserted inside), an ivory and malachite cameo, an 18-carat gold ring (size 6), a small 18-carat gold chain, a string of pearls.

Ruth wondered what it would have been like if she had been home when the burglar arrived. Would he have seen her naked? Would he have admired her breasts? Would he have thought her old? She did not think of rape or violation. She saw the burglar's hands, her mother's cameo with its bare-breasted woman carved in ivory—in his hands. And there Ruth was in the cradle of her mother's arm. But her mother is old, her hair is white. There Ruth lies, inside the crook of that old arm. Did her mother fear that she might drop her? In the mirror Ruth saw her mother's drooping, comforting breasts in her own small ones that lay against her own chest, her breasts that no longer stood. Out loud to the mirror, to the burglar, to the man who had her jewels, who could give them back if he chose, she said, "The test of time."

The burglar wore a pinstripe suit. He was college educated. He'd gone to law school. His life was like a game, entering other people's houses, neatly removing valuables, understanding something about them. He stole for fun at night, practiced law at his leisure in the daytime. He loved a married woman and did not feel the need to be faithful to her, but did not sleep with anyone else. He hadn't found anyone else he wanted to sleep with.

He decided to give the pearls to his girlfriend, to fence the rest except the locket. He didn't know what to do with the locket—identifiable, old, probably not valuable because of the crude seal. He knew jewelry and he knew the pearls were old, also not very valuable, but also not identifiable if he removed the clasp. The turquoise and gold clasp was gaudy, but at least the special clasp was a sign of a jeweler's hand in the stringing of the pearls—a good sign, a nice offering. The pearls would be his first gift. Would she take them?

She said he didn't exist. That she'd made him up.

He liked her for this ruse, this game. And he wondered if he *did* exist. He lived a double life: the law and its violation. "Who am I?" he'd sometimes ask himself when he moved from one life to the other, and then he'd laugh, for that question struck him as a joke. A question people who took themselves too seriously asked. "As if there were an answer," he'd say. He didn't need the answer to *that* question. He needed to exist.

Stealing affirmed his presence. The woman whose jewelry box he'd opened knew he existed. Of that he was sure.

The next night when Ruth got home from work, when she yelled, "Is anyone here?" Ben was in the kitchen sorting through the mail.

"I am," he said. "I'm here."

Ruth said, "'Here I am,' said Adonai."

"You're making fun of me," said Ben.

"No," Ruth said, "I'm afraid."

"Of the burglar?"

"What else?" But she wasn't afraid of the burglar. This she knew now, after she'd stood last night in front of the mirror looking at her breasts.

"We'll get a burglar alarm," said Ben.

And Ruth said, "Yes, an alarm."

And then to herself, this: What would the burglar advise?

The burglar was interested in stealing and ethics. Although he did not believe in giving to the poor, he did believe in stealing from the rich. And he wondered if he should ever give back anything he'd stolen. Become Robin Hood, revised. The burglar thought the Robin Hood of the old tale was a hypocrite. Giving to the poor—as if he were a god, as if he could right a wrong, decide what was just or unjust. The arrogance of it appalled him.

He mailed to all his friends on the Internet what he called "a personality test" about Robin Hood, Marion, Little John, and the Sheriff. He called it that because these days, everyone loved these kinds of tests that defined what they foolishly thought made them unique. He made up his test, his retelling of the story, to reveal their ethics—the story beneath their choices. What he learned made him feel he had an edge, and that edge of knowing made him feel he existed.

His message said: "Take this test. Do not cheat by looking at the answers. (He wondered how many *did* cheat; his guess was, not many.) Just write the four names down on a piece of paper and let's compare. Here's the test and, remember, this is a different sort of story from the old story you know.

"'The Sheriff of Nottingham captured Little John and Robin Hood and imprisoned them in his maximum-security dungeon. Maid Marion begged the Sheriff for their release, pleading her love for Robin. The Sheriff agreed to release them only if Maid Marion spent the night with him. To this she agreed. The next morning the Sheriff released his prisoners. Robin at once demanded that Marion tell him how she persuaded the Sheriff to let them go free. Marion confessed the truth, and was bewildered when Robin called her a slut, and said he never wanted to see her again. At this Little John defended her, inviting her to leave Sherwood with him and promising lifelong devotion. She accepted and they rode away together.'

"Now in terms of realistic everyday standards of behavior, put Robin, Marion, Little John, and the Sheriff in the order in which you consider they showed the most morality and honesty (from 'most' to 'least'). There is no 'right' answer.'''

The burglar believed this story revealed Robin Hood for what he was—a foolish, self-important moralist. That was all he needed to know. He hadn't bothered to score the test.

The married woman he loved scored the test this way: the Sheriff, Little John, Marion, and Robin.

When Ben asked Ruth to meet him at Pesce for dinner, she said, "Shouldn't we stay home?"

"Why should we stay home?" he asked her over the phone from his office to hers.

"You know why."

"Because you're afraid we'll be robbed?"

"Yes," she lied. She wanted to stay home because she thought the burglar would come again. She wanted to be there when he came.

"Let me take you out to dinner. If you get there before me, order a bottle of the French white Burgundy we like. Trust me. No one will break in tonight."

But if he'd come once, why wouldn't he come again? Because he'd gotten what he wanted, of course. This was the sensible way to think about it. And the security system was to be installed next week. Once that happened, she knew he wouldn't come again. It would be foolish, and he was a professional. She wondered if he was white or black. Tall or short. She knew he was slim: burglars must be fit to do such work, to be efficient, practical, and quick. Like Cary Grant in *To Catch a Thief*. A handsome cat burglar who would reform, return her jewels. Become her lover? She walked from the subway at Dupont Circle to Pesce on P Street and met Ben.

Ruth was eating lobster, he grouper, when he said, "Why didn't we make love this weekend?"

She didn't know. Was it because, as she thought, that he didn't really want her? Had he really tried to make love? She didn't think so. She said, "I didn't want to push it," meaning that she hadn't initiated anything. Had he? Did he think he had? Had she missed it? And why was he asking now?

He said, "I wanted to."

They had had this conversation many times in the last year. But not this way. Always before, she had been the one to ask.

At Pesce, at a different table, on a different night after work, eating clams with linguine, she'd said, "So how many men do you think got an offer like that this morning?"

He'd sat for a while and then said, "In the world or the U.S.?"

She had not answered. She was still angry from the morning rebuff even though she'd believed she'd deserved it.

He'd continued, "In the U.S., there are about 250 million people. Half are male—that's 125 million. Half of those are children or geezers—that leaves 62 million. Suppose one percent got the same offer this morning—that's 620,000 guys. Most of them are married and turned it down."

She'd laughed, her childish anger dissipated by his self-deprecation. Childish anger for just punishment. Do we ever outgrow that?

If only she'd been able to explain why, after her mother died, she'd wanted to make love all the time. Every day. She'd been ashamed that mourning increased her passion. And his rebuffs? Deserved. Deserved. She said this to herself after each rebuff, and there were many. Deserved.

Would the burglar have turned her down? This was what she thought while Ben poured more white wine into her glass. The

wine had a light greenish tint like her mother's hazel eyes, in her
mother's kitchen, when the light from the window made a kalei-
doscope, the colors of grass and sun, in her eyes. She couldn't see
her mother's face clearly. She dipped her finger into the wine and
then into her mouth to see if she could taste the color. She said,
"My mother could stretch a piece of dough across a table. Make
it so thin I could see through it. Still it was strong. An impossible
thing, don't you think?"

"A non sequitur," Ben said, "don't you think?"

And Ruth laughed. This way Ben had of making her laugh
always surprised her, made her want him. She said, "I was watching that PBS cooking show *Great Chefs*, something like that. Do
you know the show?"

He said, "Ah, the digression continues."

"I don't think it's a digression." She was mystified that he
couldn't follow her because she often spoke this way with him,
letting her thoughts fall out like dreams in the safety of sleep.

"Then probably it's not," he said. He winked at her and then
said, "I saw that."

And again she laughed. She knew he'd seen her left eyebrow
respond—in a brief arc—as it always did to whatever he subtly
did to seduce her: a brief touch on the inside of her wrist or
across her little finger, or just the words, "your hands," as if there
were no words to tell her what he saw. In response to that quirky
eyebrow, he'd often say, "Can you do that at will?" Of course, she
couldn't. And then, with that brief exchange and their laughter,
she and he both knew they'd make love. Would they make love
tonight? "Anyway," she said, "the chef stretched a piece of dough
across a table, across a thin wide cloth. Strudel dough."

"Like your mother's strudel? Is that how she made it?"

"You see, it's not a digression. You follow."

He had eaten this pastry in her mother's kitchen. "No, I don't
follow, but I did love her strudel."

When Ruth was a child she'd watched her mother lay down sliced apples and raisins, sprinkle the sugar and cinnamon, and roll the dough with an old frayed linen cloth that had been her mother's. And then the magic trick, when the cloth dropped away and one long delicate tube of dough appeared, the width of the table, and Ruth's mother cut through the layers of dough and fruit and sugar, placed the pieces on the long blackened cookie sheet that had also been her mother's. Ruth had not seen anyone do this except her mother and hadn't seen it since she was a child.

"I don't think this is a non sequitur," Ruth repeated because she was trying to explain. Oh, what was it? That whenever she thought of the burglar, her mother appeared? He'd taken her mother's jewels, hadn't he? Because she couldn't explain, and because she didn't think they'd make love, even though she knew he wanted to, even though she wanted to, she gave up. "The burglar," she heard herself say. And wanted to say, as if it would explain something: An alarm, yes, an alarm.

"The burglar and strudel. Let me think. You want to steal a dessert?" He had a menu in his hand now. The waiter had come and gone, cleared the plates. "Why don't you have the apple tart?"

"Do you think I'm losing my mind?"

"I think you miss your mother."

The burglar put on his pinstripe suit, carried his leather briefcase that he'd bought on a trip to Florence, and knocked on the door of the house he'd robbed three weeks ago. It was six in the evening, and he knew that the woman was home and the husband was not because he had watched the house for many months before the burglary. He knew what she looked like, her habits, when she went to work and came home. Though he couldn't be sure she would be there tonight, the chances were good. She came to the door wearing a blue faded apron over her silk blouse and trim black skirt. He wondered why she hadn't changed her clothes before cooking. He told her that he was on his way home, that he lived on Virgilia, that he'd received a mis-delivered letter. He said, "I take the bus and get off here so I thought I'd drop it by. I would have put it in your slot but I saw you were home." She thanked him. He found her unusually attractive, not beautiful, but with large open eyes, very light brown, almost green, brown-green, dark Atlantic Ocean eyes. He'd gone to the ocean with his parents when he was a boy, to Atlantic City and, until he'd seen clear water in the Caribbean, he'd thought all oceans must be brown-green, a color he loved but that disturbed him. Her eyes were like the Atlantic. He could not see through them, he could not tell if she knew whether he was lying, if she believed him. He could only tell that she was lis-tening closely, not dismissing him, that something about him interested her. She did not speak. She took the letter that he'd taken from the wicker basket she left on the porch (many people in Chevy Chase did this, feeling safe, wanting to make things easier for the mailman because the old houses had thin brass mail slots not suited for magazines, for junk mail). She did not look at the letter. She held it, looked at him, waited. And so he said—a non sequitur, "I used to go to Atlantic City when I was a boy."

And she said, "So did I." And then, "Why did you say that?"

"Because of your brown-green eyes."

"Hazel," she said. And then, as if she'd been thinking about just this thing, the same thing that made him look at her so closely, "I used to look into my mother's eyes and think, ocean green."

Ruth was drawn to the man in the pinstripe suit returning her mail—a well-dressed boy scout. She liked the way he stood back from the doorway, giving her space. But anyone could be danger-ous. The burglary.

The burglar had never done this before: visited the scene of the crime. It was a stupid thing to do, and he knew better, of course. Why risk his sideline, his way to get inside other people's lives? He did not get rich on what he stole, though his income was nicely supplemented. He got rich on knowing. He knew that the Wilsons in Cleveland Park did not have any jewelry though they were quite rich. He had taken nothing from their house except the knowledge that Mr. Wilson did not buy his wife these kinds of gifts. The paintings on the walls were originals—but the burglar knew that paintings were hard to fence. He believed he knew that Mr. Wilson did not love Mrs. Wilson because of the dearth of jewelry in a very rich household.

What had interested the burglar about his take from Ruth and her husband was that he thought he could discern the gifts the husband had given and the gifts someone else had given, the ones in the little white cardboard box.

But now he had to wonder—because she'd not found his non sequitur odd, not found him odd—Could she know me? Does she suspect? Can she know I've been in her bedroom, looked through her drawers, taken things that mattered to her? He did not think so, but the thought, the possibility, that what one wants to hide (or maybe does not want to hide?) could be seen by another did intrigue him. And her skin, her eyes, the openness of her face drew him to her. And then there was the question that mattered the most to him: did he exist? The burglar? The child? The lover?

Ruth went to the video store and rented *To Catch a Thief*. She watched Cary Grant at his hilltop home when the police came to question him about the burglaries being committed by someone else who was using his modus operandi (the police thought Cary was the burglar, of course). She watched Cary Grant fall in love with Grace Kelly, watched the fireworks out the window when Grace, in a strapless gown and an extravagant diamond necklace, said to Cary, "Reach out and touch them, John. You know you want them." The double entendre. The jewels. The breasts. And then, the burglar.

Ruth took a bath, filled the tub with steaming water, and pretended that when the burglar reached into the tub, he brushed her nipples while he unlatched the gold chain on her neck, while he took away her mother's wedding band (size 6) etched with the forget-me-nots, while he took the locket, the pearls, the cameo Ruth used to wear on a black velvet ribbon.

Once, when Ruth was bathing her mother, after the stroke that left her mother paralyzed on one side, her leg and arm, after she could no longer speak, after Ruth had rubbed her mother's mottled back, washed her yellowed toes and placed the washcloth in her mother's right hand to wash between her legs, between her breasts, Ruth had touched the locket. Her mother dropped the washcloth, covered Ruth's hand with hers, wrapped Ruth's fingers round the locket. Then she placed Ruth's hand on the catch at the back of the gold chain, and Ruth understood that she wanted it removed. Ruth undid the catch and held the locket in her open palm—a strand of Ruth's grandmother's hair lay inside the locket, placed there with the help of a jeweler, after Ruth's mother had taken the scissors from the drawer, after she had closed her mother's eyes, before she'd wrapped her in the shroud. In a silent giving over, Ruth's mother closed Ruth's fingers. And Ruth laid her head on her mother's wet breasts—her mother who when naked did what needed doing.

Now Ruth lay in her own bath and called out to her husband, "Ben, come bathe with me." When he opened the door, she said, "You know you want them," and placed her hands beneath her breasts. He sat on the edge of the tub and placed his hands around her head.

"Kiss me, please?" she said.

And when he opened his mouth to hers, when he took her bottom lip lightly between his teeth, she cried.

"Tell me," he said.

"The mourner's locket, the locket."

He took off his clothes and slid into the tub, wrapped his body round her, pressed his head into the back of her neck, cupped her breasts in his hands and said, "Yes, I want them."

The burglar communicated with his girlfriend—*the other married woman*, as he thought of her now—by e-mail. After his visit to Ruth's house, after the exchange of the letter, after he'd lied and become connected to this woman with her wide-open face, he wanted more than ever to believe that he existed. But his was a false life. How could he reach this woman whose jewelry he held in his hands? The jewelry he hadn't fenced yet, the jewelry he couldn't return, the pieces in the little white cardboard box that somehow he now knew must have belonged to Ruth's mother? He knew, when she'd said, "I used to look into my mother's eyes," that her mother must be dead, that he'd taken something that hurt her more than the loss of valuables. Seeing the woman he'd stolen from made him unreal—he couldn't tell her who he was.

Could his girlfriend, who told him all the time he didn't exist, help? Could giving her the pearls help? For the first time in many years, he wanted to sleep with another woman, with the woman in the silk blouse, black skirt, faded apron, the woman who gently accepted his non sequitur about his trips to Atlantic City, the woman who made him remember when he was a child, the ingenuous, open-faced woman—this woman, whom he wanted to affirm him. And she had, hadn't she? She had affirmed him with those words about her mother's eyes. In his head he heard "ocean-green," and sent this e-mail to his girlfriend: "I have a gift from the ocean for you. This gift will make you believe I exist. See me today at lunch. Meet me at the Washington Hotel, on Fifteenth Street, in the lobby."

She wrote back: "How can I take a gift from you? How would I explain it? I'll meet you at noon. But remember that you don't exist. And because you don't exist, you can give me nothing to hold in my hand, to take home. Now tell me: how did you score the test?"

Why should he score the test? He'd made it up. That's what he told his friends who'd asked. It was harder to refuse his girl-friend—he needed her. So he considered Marion—or was it the woman whose jewelry he'd stolen? She was first on his list. Robin Hood last. He didn't much care about Little John and the Sheriff, thought them interchangeable, but saw no need to tell his girlfriend that. He wrote back: "Marion, Little John, the Sheriff, Robin. See you at noon." Then he called the hotel and booked a room.

When his girlfriend was standing in her pink silk camisole, while she was unzipping her skirt, he placed Ruth's pearls around her neck. His girlfriend took off all her clothes, made love to him wearing the pearls, and then gave the pearls back to him. She said, "If I take them, how would I explain them to my husband?"

"Say you bought them in an antique jewelry store."

"With cash, with a check, with a credit card? He keeps all the bills. He would wonder how I did this without spending any money. I would have to pay you for the pearls."

"Would I exist then? If you paid me for them?"

"Yes. You would be Robin Hood."

"But that explains nothing," he said, because he was thinking of the Robin Hood who stole from the rich and gave to the poor. "What do you mean?" he asked.

"It means you would exist," she said, "but you would be at the bottom of my list." She folded his fingers around the pearls in his open palm. "And yours."

What was this game she was playing? The burglar tried to discern his girlfriend's logic—and his own, for he had not allowed her to pay him for the pearls. He decided that his girlfriend was telling him that his existence came at a cost. He'd have to pay for it.

He deduced this through a syllogism: a man tries to prove that he exists by stealing pearls from one married woman and giving them to another married woman. The second married woman, who is his lover, insists on paying for them. If he accepts the money, she is able to deceive her husband. Therefore, the man would pay for his existence with deception.

The burglar had no problem with the equation: deception equals existence. It suited him, his choices, the stealing. Why then had he not taken the money? The other married woman was the reason, of course. She was the missing link in his syllogism. Did he exist with her? He had deceived her. He would have to see her again.

Ben made love to Ruth after their bath, but she, for the first time in the last year, felt no desire for him. She could think only of the burglar, her mother—her mother, the burglar. She could not relax, she could not concentrate, she could not reach climax. She believed she'd failed Ben because she wanted the burglar. When they were done, she slept and dreamed.

She is in a house with a woman with a beautiful baby. The woman with the baby is ill, lying in a bed. Ruth takes the baby in her arms, bares her breasts as if she might feed the baby, but she is not with milk, so she uses her small breasts to comfort the baby. The burglar enters. He is the man Ruth wants. He approaches her. She does not cover her breasts, but speaks to him as if they are covered. She watches his eyes at the sight of her breasts and the baby. She asks him naively—for she knows the answer—"Have we ever kissed?" "No," he says before he slowly leans towards her, his hands open in that unknowing, awkward way a man opens his hands to touch a woman's breasts because the touch, the thought of it, arouses him. Ingenuous. Without intent. Ruth wants him to touch her breasts. But instead he kisses her, cradles her head with his hands and the softness of the kiss, the restraint he exercises in not touching her bare and vulnerable breasts, increases her desire for him.

At breakfast Ruth said to Ben, "It's the burglar's fault."

"What is?"

"I can't lie about it anymore. It's the burglar."

He took both her hands in his across the table, held them for a moment, and then placed each of her hands—so gently he did this—first one hand on the side of his head, then the other, so that they were both leaning on the table and she was cradling his head.

With his gesture, so tender, so concerned, she became alarmed. All she could think was: *What have I done?*

"Ruth, talk to me, please."

His face was so close to hers she could breathe him in, and with each breath of him, she felt safer, but still she couldn't explain. "He's on my mind." That was all she could think to say.

"Okay, he's on your mind. What's his fault?" And still, his face close to hers, his hands over hers, his hands pressing on hers. Did he think if he held her close enough to him he could make her better?

"My failure." No, she wasn't going to cry. Not over this, not over making love, or not making love. Certainly not over her failure to reach climax. She pulled back from Ben.

He kept one of his hands on top of hers on the table. "And when did you fail?"

Had she? Her dream came to mind. Maybe she hadn't failed by not reaching climax. Maybe Ben had failed by not touching her as the burglar touched, or rather did not touch, her in her dream. But now, the way, when she was awake, the burglar and her mother came to mind together, she recalled the mother and the baby in the dream. She recalled the last time she'd laid her head on her mother's naked breast, when she was a grown woman, and that her mother died soon after. She said, not really understanding the dream, but knowing now something more about it, "I dreamed about my mother last night—and the burglar." Could she tell Ben about her desire for the burglar? Which made no sense at all, but if she didn't ever talk about it, how would she figure it out? So she said, "I thought about him when we were making love."

"And were you afraid?" Ben asked.

"Afraid of what?" What could she possibly be afraid of? Ben's question made no sense to her. She was confessing, and he was asking her if she was afraid.

"Afraid that we'd be robbed?"

"We have been robbed."

Ben laughed. Why was he laughing?

"This is not a laughing matter." But she began to laugh too without knowing why.

"Then why are you laughing?" he asked.

"You first," she said.

"Because you're funny," he said and put his face, his mouth, and his nose inside her palm as if he could breathe her in. And maybe he could, she thought. "Because you're you," he continued. "Because you speak in non sequiturs. Because sometimes I can even follow them. Because I love you. Your turn."

She kissed the inside of his palm and told, "Well, what if I don't deserve a climax? What if I can never have one again? What if I never want to make love to you again?" And of course she didn't deserve to climax—all those months after her mother had died when she had wanted sex. What had been wrong with her?

"And why would any of these things ever be true?"

"The burglar." She knew it was his fault. But what did he have to do with any of this? With what she deserved?

He looked at her as if he had the answer. "I think I'm going to have to get this guy. It's the only solution. Get out of Dodge, cowboy. Ben is here. I am."

And now Ruth laughed again and said, "'Here I am,' said Adonai."

"You know," said Ben, "that's not funny."

"Of course not. I'm sorry. It's just that you keep saying that. 'Here I am.'" She went to him, sat on his lap. "Okay, get the burglar for me. Get him."

The burglar removed the turquoise and gold catch from the string of pearls. He was going to fence them along with the cameo, the gold ring with the forget-me-nots, and all the husband's gifts—the earrings and bracelets that had been in the woman's jewelry box. But what to do with the locket that lay alone now in the rubbed cotton in the little white cardboard box? He put the locket in the pocket of his pinstripe suit, threw away the cardboard box.

What do I need this for? he asked himself. Is it some sort of memento? As if I'd ever give anything back.

He put the rest of the jewelry into his briefcase and went to see his fence. While he haggled, while he exchanged the jewelry for a mere $250, he fingered the locket in his pocket.

He took the subway to Bethesda and walked the mile and a half to Chevy Chase, to Ruth's house, to figure out what she had to do with him, with his equation: deception equals existence. What did she have to do with his need to prove that he existed? Maybe he would have an affair with her, the ultimate deception? To steal and then to possess? This was the way to affirm his existence. He was not thinking about the time, about when the husband would arrive. He was thinking about the woman. He was careless in his desire to see her again, the missing link in his syllogism.

She came to the door in black leggings and a sweat shirt. No apron. She'd changed her clothes. He looked at his watch. The husband will be coming soon. He knew this because she'd taken the time to change her clothes, because he knew their schedule. But all the better. I'll seduce her before he gets here. He liked working on a deadline. He liked stealing.

Ruth wondered why the well-dressed boy scout had returned. "More misdelivered mail?" she asked.

"No." He stepped back to look at her, at her ocean-green eyes. He knew he needed to speak, allay fear, do something deceptive. Instead he said, "I'm worried." Because he was, though he wasn't sure why or why this woman caused him to speak his mind.

Ruth said, "Are you all right?" She was standing with the door partially open. She could close it at any time. She did think about closing it, but the man looked distressed, as if he had something to tell her, as if something were wrong. He did not look dangerous. But she thought, Anyone could be. The burglary. I should close the door.

He said, "I know you don't know me. I know this is odd. But remember when you talked about your mother? About Atlantic City? Or maybe that's what I talked about."

She simply couldn't close the door. The mention of her mother. "My mother died almost a year ago. I think about her all the time. I talk about her to strangers. I probably said something about her to you. I've been doing and saying odd things ever since she died. I don't know. Maybe I've always said and done odd things." And now she spoke her mind, "I should be afraid of you, I think. I should shut the door, shouldn't I?" Her mother, the burglar. What should she do? Certainly not shut the door on this sad, bemused man who'd returned her mail.

"Yes, you should. Why don't you? I'll go away. I should go away." This gentle, sad woman. How could he ever know her? What did she have to do with him? Nothing. Nothing. Nothing. And then he heard himself say this out loud. "Nothing. Nothing." She must think he was mad. "I'm so sorry to have bothered you."

"Why are you worried?" Ruth asked.

The burglar heard Ben's car pull into the driveway. He knew he'd timed this all wrong. He must go now. But he stood trans-fixed by her, by her question. He couldn't possibly tell her about his syllogism, about the pearls. He said, "Would you tell me something about your mother?"

Ben drove the car into the garage, got his briefcase out of the trunk, pulled the garage door down. The garage was not con-nected to the house. So he had to walk down the driveway and up the path to the house. All this took time, time the burglar needed.

On seeing Ben, Ruth said, "When my husband fixed my mother's heating pad—it was a large heating pad because she had a back problem before she became very ill—this was a long time before she died. When he fixed it, she said, 'Golden hands. He has golden hands. Marry him.' As if she knew. How could she know?" Why was Ruth asking this of the man? Why was she thinking of the burglar? There he was again—his hand brushing her breast, removing the locket. Because she was talking about her mother. That was it. And because all this made some sort of quirky sense to her, she said to the man in the pinstripe suit, "We were robbed."

The burglar was alarmed. Could she know? He put his hand in his pocket and held the locket.

The man in the pinstripe suit was now staring at her oddly. And why not? She was behaving oddly. "I'm speaking in non sequiturs again. I'm silly. I'm sorry. Oh, my husband." And then, "That's why I talk about my mother, you see." She was trying to explain the unexplainable.

But the burglar believed he understood. He said, "And you lost something of your mother's?" He believed he existed when he said this. And to affirm his existence, and to be sure she understood him, he added, "When you were robbed, I mean." He couldn't have the woman, but he had her story now, didn't he? He knew the way her mother knew.

"Yes. No. I don't know. Did I?" Ruth said. Ben was coming toward her.

That morning, he'd awakened her when he'd laid his head in the crook of her neck, kissed her there and on her face, little kisses, the way she'd kissed their infant daughter who was grown now, gone away. She'd smelled baby powder in his hair, but knew there was none. And there she was in the crook of her mother's arm, again. "If I could remember," she'd said. And Ben had kissed her on the mouth. "What?" he asked. She didn't answer. She remembered. The scent of skin, her mother's, her daughter's, Ben's.

She said to the man in the pinstriped suit, "No."

Now Ben stood between the burglar and Ruth. He looked at Ruth.

Ruth wondered what he saw. Why was she talking to a strange man about her mother? How would she explain this?

The burglar wondered what he saw. The burglar wanted Ruth.

Ruth wanted her mother, Ben, and the burglar. But who was the burglar? Who was this strange man? She didn't know. She wanted to lay her head on her mother's breast. She needed to be alone with Ben. She needed the man in the pinstripe suit to go away.

The burglar knew that Ben could tell that he wanted his wife. He knew because Ben had stepped between the two of them. He had his back to the burglar. He stood facing his wife. He showed the burglar that he was this woman's man. He blocked the burglar's sight, his eyes on hers.

When Ben moved in front of Ruth, she noticed that he was wearing the gray solid tie with his dark blue suit. She said, "You're wearing the gray solid tie." The tie, the white shirt, the way he looked at her, the way he stood between her and the man in the pinstripe suit made her want him. Cary Grant came to mind. "Cary Grant always wore a solid tie, did you know that?" The movie *To Catch a Thief* came to mind—the way Cary seduced Grace. Or was it Grace who seduced Cary? She laughed. She was feeling oddly erotic. This strange man who looked at her eyes. Her mother. Her husband. The burglar. She said to Ben, "You know you want them." She did not touch her breasts, but she laughed. And she could tell that he remembered. Ben said to Ruth, "Here I am," and he laughed.

Ruth laid her head on his chest. "Yes, here you are." She missed her mother's breasts. Her naked mother, straightening the linen closet, changing a light bulb, bathing her child, giving over the locket that was now lost—that efficient, practical woman. Death had taken her mother. And Ruth wanted to make love.

The burglar knew these two would make love.

He put his hand in his pocket, turned the locket in his palm. He knew the locket was old, that it must have belonged to Ruth's mother, that it could not be replaced. He wouldn't give it back. He couldn't fence it and he couldn't give it to his girl-friend. He would keep it. He was no Robin Hood. (Or was he? he asked himself.)

He walked to the subway. He didn't know if he existed or not. But the woman with the ocean-green eyes, the gentle woman who disturbed him? He knew that she existed.

When Ruth lay down with Ben that night, her naked breasts against his chest, she said again, "Here you are."

Rugalach

I'm named for my grandmother, who died before I was born. Her recipes are in my mother's three-ring binder, where the past is written down in cups of sugar and pinches of salt: soup with kreplach, coarse chopped liver, and rugalach.

The recipe for rugalach—a cream cheese and butter pastry filled with raisins, jam, and nuts, covered with cinnamon and sugar—is put down in more detail than most, including the two tablespoons of sour cream that make the difference. My mother's pastries were born from the quick, solid pressure of her arms on dough that rolled out like unraveling tissue. She used her mother's wooden rolling pin and board, darkened with flour and butter.

The first time I tried to make the pastry, when I was married with children of my own, the dough stuck to the board as the fat softened with the heat of my effort. My mother said, "Cover the board with cinnamon and sugar, more than you think you need. That'll keep it from sticking." But I didn't have her arms, made strong with scrubbing the white marble steps of her house in East Baltimore, where she grew up and where she came back to live when my grandmother was dying.

My mother never spoke of the burden of that time. She told me instead the story of her mother's journey from Latvia when just a girl. "Your age," she said to me when I was just fourteen. "Imagine that. Traveling all alone with one valise. Leaving her parents behind. Her marriage to your grandpa was arranged by a cousin who'd also gotten out."

I found it hard indeed to imagine all these things. I even hated going to camp. Arranged marriages were just beyond belief.

"My father was a good man, but tough," she'd say. Then she'd look away as her eyes softened with thoughts of her mother. "Ah, she was an angel." She'd turn that memory-warmed gaze on me. "What a name you have," she'd say. And so my grandmother's sweetness spread across me like a veil. An undeserved gift.

I had to make her rugalach for Rosh Hashanah. I bought a marble pastry board that holds the chill on the dough long enough for me to make the thin circle of pastry that I then cut into eight wedges according to the diagram scrawled at the end of the recipe. "Remember to roll the crescents in more cinnamon and sugar before they go on the baking sheet," my mother advised.

And each year she graded the rugalach. "Almost." "A little small." "Roll the dough out thinner next year." Or, "Use more cinnamon in your mixture." "Be sure to pull the ends in a curl to get a good crescent shape." My father was the ultimate judge. "You're getting there," he said a few years before she died.

And then I became obsessed with knishes. I can still taste the crisp dough as it cracked open in my mouth, the spices tingling on my tongue. My mother's dough was like rice paper that she cut in squares filled with shredded, cooked brisket, seasoned with lots of salt and pepper and flecked with roasted potato. She folded the dough into pouches like little Chinese dumplings, but smaller and round, with the edges swirled down in the center like a belly button. These were nothing like the heavy concoctions in glass deli counters these days, filled with potato or spinach and called knishes. As I bit into one of these gut-bomb pastries one day, I realized my mother's knishes were obsolete.

I scrolled through the recipe binder. "Sour Cream Schnecken," "Mollye's Milkadich Buns," "Besse's Noodle Kugle." More recipes I'd never made, more family trademarks. The order of the recipes, a mystery.

And then I found "Knish Dough." Below the list of ingredients were these words: "Mix tog. and work dough. (Meat, salt, pepper. Grind meat, gribiness, mashed potatoes all tog.)" What, pray tell, was gribiness? I stood in the middle of my Chevy Chase kitchen with copper pots hanging from my ceiling, a Cuisinart sitting powerfully on my counter ready to act as meat grinder, a brisket in the self-cleaning oven, and I cried over the word *gribiness*.

My mother cooked in a narrow white kitchen, like her mother's, in a brick row house. Her apron smelled of garlic and starch. When she opened the oven door, I saw black and white speckled porcelain walls and felt the wave of roasted heat.

This is where I told her how my fourth grade teacher made me stand outside the class. How I'd been unjustly accused of running in the hall. How I couldn't stop crying. My first experience with public shame. This is where she pulled me to her heavy bosom and let me lay my head.

Her hands moved quickly from cutting board to frying pan. Onions sizzling in the pan 'til they were nearly burned. The smell watered in my mouth for what I knew would come. This is where the holy days began.

And that's how I remembered what to do. I fried onions and bits of chicken skin with their clinging yellow layers of fat that melted in the pan, leaving fragrant cracklings. I seasoned the burnished cracklings and crispy onions with kosher salt and fresh pepper and ground them with cooked brisket in my Cuisinart in the hope that I had deciphered gribiness through the haze of memory.

I rolled the little pouches filled with meat, browned them in a thin film of Crisco in the oven on one of her old cookie sheets, blackened now with use and age. My pouches were a bit mis-shapened and the dough not thin enough. I set my holiday table with her silver and her crystal and waited for my father to arrive for Rosh Hashanah dinner.

Before the meal, I served the knishes in the living room to my husband, who remembered well my mother's cooking, to my grown children—one who popped the pastry in his mouth with no comment, the other abstaining in reverence to a vegetarian diet. My husband relished his. And then my father said, "You take me back," as he reached for another and looked over at my mother's youthful picture on the bookshelf.

In the picture her hair is dark and wavy like my grandmother's, whose picture sits nearby. My grandmother who traveled here alone with strangers, who never again saw the parents who'd saved her from a pogrom by sending her away. And I thought of when my mother, an old woman, cried out for her as she faced death. My grandmother whose recipes come alive in my hands.

Guarding the Pie

Martin had kissed her during the week of shiva, barely five days after they'd stood beside his father's grave. Now with her own father close to death, Rachel wondered how he could have done it. Not that she excused herself, either—Martin's father was her uncle; Martin, her first cousin.

When Martin called, it had been thirty years since they'd been alone together, when they'd been briefly—over almost before it began—engaged. They'd seen each other, of course, occasionally at family parties, bar and bat mitzvahs.

He said, "I want to bring you the letters." The love letters, she understood without his telling her, the ones she had written him.

He was calling from Boston, where he lived. He told her he was coming to Baltimore to see his eighty-four-year-old mother—the same age as Rachel's father. "She's still on her own, thank goodness," said Martin, "but I know I need to see her more often now." Rachel didn't mention that her father wasn't faring as well. "I'll be coming in about three weeks," he said. "I could drop by one afternoon." So there'd be time to cancel, for her to change her mind, for him to change his.

"Why now?" she asked. "What do I want with the letters?"

When he didn't answer, while his silence gave her time to

think, she decided this must be his way of telling her he'd kept them all this time. Well, he had, hadn't he? She felt flattered, though ashamed to admit it. She agreed to the visit because he'd saved the letters.

She hung up and sat at the kitchen table with her husband, who'd been reading the Sunday *Sun*, eating his second, late-morning bagel, drinking coffee. "I think I should see him alone, don't you?"

"Not really." Al rubbed the balding spot on the crown of his head, the way he did when he was feeling uncomfortable, when he didn't want to explain how he was feeling.

"Don't tell me you're jealous. There's nothing to be jealous about. It was years ago. It was nothing." That was not true. But how could she tell Al, who, after all these years, would sneak up behind her and with a flirt in his voice, say "stick person," and kiss her on her thin neck—how could she tell him that even now she could close her eyes and feel the promise of Martin's kiss?

Al continued to rub his head. She took his hand from that place he scratched, from the tiny scabs, the visible evidence of his discomfort—punishment inflicted on himself, perhaps, for his inability to speak his mind? The gesture, as if it were a reproach, always made her stop and consider what she'd just said. "Think of it as unfinished business," she added, telling him the truth now.

For she had always loved Martin.

"Umm," Al grunted.

When she was five and Martin was ten, she had loved him. When she was ten and he fifteen, when she was sixteen, seventeen, eighteen, when she was nineteen and he was twenty-four, she had loved him. It was a childish love, a crush. But when she was twenty, when he buried his father, when he kissed her on the mouth, told her that he loved her too, she thought he had waited for her, the way no one else would ever do again. The impropriety of the kiss, its urgency, its passion mixed with mourning, made it seem profound.

"Ancient history," she said, for that's what it was, wasn't it?

Al's hand went up to that spot on his head again. She'd given him something to worry about. But he was so laconic she often read too much into what he didn't say.

Still, she felt a tug of betrayal when she wrote the date—not on the kitchen calendar with the Goldsteins' Bat Mitzvah in January, dinner with the Rosenbergs Wednesday night, *Tosca* at the Washington opera in two weeks, the Orioles at Camden Yards in April—but in her personal date book, the one she carried with her.

She'd been thinking about betrayal lately. It seemed to be all around her, everywhere she looked, a part of everyday life, nothing out of the ordinary. On every daytime talk show—not the sort of shows she watched, of course. But every now and then, surfing through the channels, looking for a cooking show, hoping for Julia Child, she would be stopped by the voices of young people explaining adultery to Ricki Lake or Sally Jesse Raphael, or some other "famous" TV host whose name would soon be forgotten by the world of unfaithful viewers. "What could I do?" a young woman could be heard saying. "It was love, true love." What drivel, Rachel would think and switch the station in search of anything on PBS.

That evening Al and Rachel's son called at their time for catching up, though usually Rachel placed the call. "Why is he calling collect?" Al said when he heard Rachel accept the charges. Daniel was, after all, twenty-five and married.

"Katya is leaving me," Daniel bluntly announced.

Al laid his head on her shoulder, snuggled in her neck as if he were about to tell her how much he loved her, and Rachel felt a tingle of arousal with her back against his chest before he mumbled, "A degree from Dartmouth, a good job, and he wants us to pay for the call?" Daniel tended to call collect when something was wrong—a signal that he needed Rachel the way he did in college when he was homesick. But Al was still paying off bills from the wedding, though Rachel had prepared most of the food for the reception herself. Why, she'd made everything except the cake. But then the flowers, the dress, the veil, Daniel's tuxedo, the kitchen helpers and servers, the rabbi—Al had been appalled at how much it could cost to be sanctioned by God. When Al complained about Rabbi Bloomberg's $1500 fee, Rachel said "Well, you don't get to smash a crystal glass for nothing, you know."

"Leaving you? Why?" She waited for an explanation. But there was no understanding this. Katya and Daniel had been married two years ago. The wedding took place in Al and Rachel's living room. Al and Rachel had flown Katya's mother from Hungary; a devout Catholic, she'd divorced Katya's father when Katya was two and vowed never to remarry. The rabbi and Father Anderson (the liberal Catholic priest who'd been hard for Katya and Daniel to find) took turns in the ecumenical ceremony. Katya's mother, who spoke no English, stood solemn-faced. Was she bemused? Distressed? Rachel had read a poem Katya chose and was trying to remember it while Daniel talked and talked without explaining.

"She's going to Italy for a week with some guy she knows from work." Katya was a graphic artist. "She says I don't pay enough attention to her." Rachel heard in his voice the little boy who used to tell her all his secrets, until he turned twelve and began to drift away from her. "She says I'm lousy in bed." What was she supposed to say to that? She already knew more about Katya and Daniel's sex life than she would have liked—and it was her own fault. Katya had spent the last year confiding in her, complaining about Daniel. Rachel listened, hoping to bond with her daughter-in-law, remembering her mother's advice—learned from her mother who'd learned it from hers—that the best way to keep your son was to love his wife. "I'm miserable," Daniel said. "I think I need to go to Italy. I need to follow her, but I don't know where the hell she is."

"Come home," Rachel said. She could barely speak. Worst of all, she'd known Katya had been thinking about going to Italy. Should she have told Daniel?

Once Rachel gave Al the story, he said, "I think Daniel should get mad."

Three weeks later, after Daniel had come home, after Katya had returned from Italy, after Daniel had flown back to Seattle to meet her, Rachel stood in her kitchen waiting for Martin to arrive. She remembered Daniel's phone call—how could she forget it?—and the one before it when she'd made a sort of date with Martin—for, she realized, that's how she'd been thinking about it. Like a silly schoolgirl. Rachel wondered how Al would feel when he found out she didn't tell him today was the day that Martin was coming.

Martin was short, shorter even than Rachel remembered. He was fifty-five, with graying curly hair. He'd let his hair grow longer than when she had loved him, when he'd kept it cut close to his scalp to hide the kinky curls that now framed his wizened, yellow face. He'd always looked old to her. Perhaps it was the olive tone of his skin like the grave dark faces of the characters in Lawrence Durrell's novels of betrayal, characters who uttered wise things ordinary people never said. Rachel remembered a line from one of those novels she'd read when she was in her twenties and still young enough to be mesmerized by the lush philosophical prose: *Truth is what most contradicts itself.*

Martin took her hand. "You're still as thin as ever."

His hand felt small compared to Al's. Delicate. Martin was a dentist and had always had skilled hands that built model air-planes, molded tiny figurines in art class. She could see him mak-ing moldings for her teeth. The thought of Martin's hands inside her mouth reminded her of the gold inlays she'd recently needed to save two teeth from root canals. She was in need of repair there and everywhere—hardly as she'd always been.

"I'm old like you, Martin," she said. "Finally, I've caught up." Rachel could see love handles beneath Martin's snug turtleneck, at the top edges of his trousers. He didn't look as fit as she'd expected. He'd been short but athletic when they were young, always talking of hiking somewhere in the woods, or up some mountain, making Rachel tired just to listen.

Martin leaned against the wood banister in her hallway, hands in his pockets, one foot across the other at the ankle, the toe of his tasseled leather loafer tipped rakishly at the floor. Posing, admiring her. "You've not a wrinkle on you."

Rachel had her mother's ivory white skin, and Martin had his father's dark exotic color. Rose and Abe, both dead now, had been deeply affectionate siblings—Rose, the youngest of the eight children, and Abe, the second oldest.

Rose had gone every day to Abe and his wife Martha's apart-ment to relieve Martha, a registered nurse, from the tedium of caring for Abe after he'd come home from the hospital to die of the cancer in his pancreas. That was the way Abe wanted it and, while he starved toward death, getting frailer, thinner every day, the two women tended him and one another.

Rachel remembered standing at the window of her home on Grantley Road in Baltimore, watching her mother outside the house in her car with her head against the steering wheel. She could see her mother's arms wrapped around the wheel, could see the sadness in her back, knew that she was weeping. But Rachel's mother didn't talk about her grief. She simply bore it, composing herself before she came inside to fix their dinner.

"And what about all this white hair?" Rachel turned from Martin's glance, walked toward the kitchen, thinking of her mother's white hair, of her mother's goodness in the face of death, Abe's, the deaths of all her brothers and sisters. Rose had died of a stroke the year before Daniel's wedding. Rachel missed her, still needed her.

Martin followed Rachel to the kitchen, where she stood in front of the cherry pie she'd set on the counter to cool. "Your hair is striking."

More compliments. What does he have in mind? "How's Judith?" she asked as a counter move. When Martin married Judith some time after he turned forty—she and Al weren't invited to the wedding; maybe they eloped; Rachel wasn't even sure about that—she'd thought: *Well, that should settle it. He's gone, married, like me.*

"Judith is Judith," Martin answered.

How was she supposed to know what that meant? She barely knew Judith. She didn't want him to see the pie. She said, "Why don't you go into the living room and have a seat. I'll bring us tea, coffee?" She didn't wait for his answer. "Go on, now," pushing forward the air in front of her, motioning him away. "Make yourself at home."

Alone in the kitchen, she thought about how things had spiraled out of control that morning when Rachel had foolishly told her daughter about the pie. When the phone rang, she'd been sure it was Martin thinking better of the visit. But it was Miriam, wanting to talk again about James. "He's not going to commit, Mom. I know you adore him, but you're going to have to forget him."

Rachel didn't answer when Miriam paused for the expected response, the way Rachel would usually say, "Of course, dear, you're right," and then dreamily add something like, "Oh, that time he grated the lemon peel for you," as if she knew what

Miriam was thinking, giving Miriam the opener, the tiny lever, that let her talk about him without admitting her need to do just that. Rachel was caught up in Martin's pending visit, saying to herself, *I thought I'd forgotten Martin.* He was gone, poof, like magic, like a memory trick.

"Mom, are you listening?"

That was when she'd said something about the pie, trying to focus on Miriam and James—or rather on "Miriam and no James." Oh, which is it? she'd been thinking, and then, heard herself making small talk about pie. Innocent enough, you'd think, but Miriam locked on—like an F-111 bomber and its target.

"Who are you baking for?" Miriam asked. "A pie means company, no?" Rachel tried to avoid answering, said something about the sour cherries that appeared once a year in late June, how she'd pitted and frozen them, something about how nice it is to have cherry pie in January. She didn't say that when she'd taken the cherries from the freezer, when she'd taken the marble pastry board—ever ready to hold the chill on dough—from her backup refrigerator in the basement, when she'd put the flour into her food processor, cut the cold butter up into little pieces and made the dough for the crust, she'd been thinking that a homemade piece of pie would ease the visit. She didn't say how nervous she was feeling. Why, she couldn't possibly tell Miriam it was Martin who was coming. Then: *What am I thinking? Nothing's going on between Martin and me. Of course, I can tell.* "My cousin Martin's coming for a visit."

"The one you almost married?"

Rachel didn't answer. Here was Miriam stating the fact of the matter—a fact Rachel didn't want to hear out loud.

"What gives?"

Exactly. What indeed? "Miriam, it's a family visit, an obligation."

"There's got to be more to it than that. After all this time? Tell me, tell me." Miriam giggled, "Mom, tell me, come on."

Rachel tried to fend Miriam off. "Martin is doing his duty." Yes, that's what this visit is about. He's finally realized he owes some explanation.

"Oh, don't think you're going to get off that easy, Mom."

Rachel took the phone from her ear and gave it a look she wished Miriam could see, a look that said, well, I certainly hope so. What was it with her children? Family intimacy run amuck? She was closer to Miriam than to Daniel. Miriam believed absolutely that Rachel could read her mind. Now Miriam was reading hers. Rachel said, "Miriam, worry about your own love life."

James and Miriam, living in Manhattan in separate apartments after their college romance, had been planning marriage when James announced he was seeing someone else. Miriam reported he'd said, "I'll always love you. You're the one." She'd said, "Mom, can you believe that? He expects me to wait this out?" Rachel agreed Miriam should move on, but in fact, both of them were stuck on James and talked incessantly about him, Rachel openly hoping he would come to his senses and Miriam wishing the same but lecturing Rachel about the reality neither had accepted.

"Ah, so you admit it," Miriam persisted. "It's a tryst, an old flame come for a visit. Will Dad be home?"

"Well, what difference does that make?"

Miriam was still giggling and, by then, so was Rachel. "Miriam, you're making me feel like an old fool."

And here Rachel stood guarding her cherry pie. She wasn't sure he deserved it. She didn't trust him. What was he doing here after all these years? She had her life well in order, had almost forgotten those bleak months when she wrote letter after letter to him in Alaska, where he was stationed in the Air Force. All those letters and no response. Now he sat in her living room and she stood deciding the fate of her pie.

"How's your father?" Martin was standing in the doorway of the kitchen.

How long had she been staring at the pie, how long had he sat alone in the living room wondering when she would appear? She hadn't put on the water. She was in a dilemma: to serve the pie or not?

Martin had moved into safe territory with the question about her father. She walked with him into the living room, forgetting about the water for coffee or tea, leaving the question of the pie undecided.

She had two high-backed red wing chairs. They looked formal, but they reclined with a push on the arms and back. When they were upright, no one would even think to guess their secret. It was always such a lovely gift to dear friends to show them how they could put their feet up while they chatted. She would bring from the kitchen a glass of wine and her homemade paté, perhaps, on the slices of French bread she'd toasted ahead of time in the oven, setting everything on a little plate on the small side table by the chair.

She decided not to tell Martin about the chair's secret when he sat down in one of them.

She sat across from him on the navy blue love seat that picked up the bit of blue in the swirling red Ahar rug, the first thing she and Al bought for the room and the only thing in the room for five years because it had taken their whole furniture budget. "Oh, I don't know," she began. "He's old, forgetful." And then she blurted out, wondering where it came from after she said it, "Everyone looks at him and thinks about death. It even happens to me sometimes. Well, all the time actually."

"So, things are not so good?" Martin was sincerely concerned. He used to go to Colt games with Rachel's father—Sam and Abe had season tickets and took along Martin and his younger brother or whoever else could go from the family in Baltimore. Martin hadn't seen Sam in years, not since Rose's funeral. His visits home were rare.

"Well, no. Yes. Oh, I don't know. He's going to be eighty-five next month. He's old. He's wearing out." Rachel studied the rug where she and Al, dear sweet Al, would dance sometimes when they were alone, to Nelson Riddle's arrangements for Frank Sinatra of "What'll I Do," of "Someone to Watch Over Me," songs her mother used to hum.

Someone to watch over me, yes, that's what we're all looking for. Someone like Al who, when they'd first gotten married, had taken over her checkbook, where each month ended with her balance correction and these words: "adjustment for March (April, etc.)." He'd carefully corrected all the balances and then told her that he didn't know why, but he loved her for all those adjustments. And, when they'd bought the rug she was now staring at, when the Iranian salesman unfurled it from the rolls stacked against the wall of the store, when she'd turned her back to hide her expression, when she had been about to blow any hope of negotiating the price, after Al stepped in front of her to see what was going on, when she'd mouthed, barely whispered, "It makes my heart beat," and fluttered her hands across her chest so he would understand, it was Al who had looked at the salesman and said, "My wife is feeling a bit uncertain. We'd like to shop around." After they'd left the store and Rachel had a chance to compose herself, it was Al who went back and bought it for her.

"And his wife?" Martin continued. "Tell me about her."

"Oh, you really need to meet Celia." Rachel's father had recently remarried. He'd met Celia, ten years his junior, at the Pikesville Senior Center where he went to play pool. "Won't you be here for a few days? You should go over. You know my father would love to see you."

"So they're happy?"

"Happy? Well, all Celia talks about is sex. 'Don't underestimate your father,' she says in her deep Peruvian accent. 'He comes through. I can attest to that,' she says." Rachel tried her best to use a Spanish accent.

Martin laughed. "What a way to go," he said, too predictably for Rachel's taste.

"Well, I'd rather not hear about it." In her memory, Martin was so sensitive, so perceptive. Couldn't he see she had a bit of trouble with this? After all, her mother and father had been married fifty-five years.

"Hmm, I guess if it were my father... Well, I'm glad my mother's doing so well, barely needs me, though I guess that could change."

"Well, Celia takes good care of him." And then to herself: *Defending her, am I? I suppose I should.* What's she done wrong? It was her father, his memory failing from hardening of the arteries, who was sleeping with another woman. Sometimes he even called Celia "Mama," to Celia's and Rachel's horror—for that was what he used to call Rose. Not that Rachel begrudged him a second chance, not that she even resented the sex. Clearly not all the arteries were failing. But goodness, he could at least tell Celia to keep it to herself. More than once, Rachel jokingly said to Celia, "As happy as I am for you, dear, no details, please," but to no avail.

She adjusted the pillows in the corners of the loveseat. Why, her father was probably sitting on a couch at the senior center talking to Celia before Mama died. After her stroke, that's where he went to get away from the tedium of care, from the painful vigil he kept, watching her drift away. Rachel had even found the senior center for him. Goodness, she'd probably helped him do it. She stared at the rug again. "Betrayal, it's everywhere," she heard herself say out loud.

"What?" said Martin.

Rachel didn't answer. She was thinking about Martin, who sat here in her house, reminding her of the past, of the fact that she'd never understood why he'd stopped writing after he'd gone back to Alaska, after what had happened to them—the kiss, their engagement—during that week of shiva after Martin's father had died. Why, she ought to accuse him the way Daniel should accuse Katya. She surprised herself with this. What exactly would Rachel accuse Martin of after all these years? Now, what Katya had done to Daniel—that was worth an accusation—at the very least—wasn't it? Al was right. Daniel should get mad. It was only natural.

"Rachel?" Martin said.

"Really, Martin, don't you see it?"

"See what?"

But she wasn't about to tell Martin Daniel's troubles, or anything about what she now referred to as "the cake incident."

Katya had finally called Daniel from somewhere in Tuscany, but wouldn't give enough information for Daniel to figure out how to follow her. So he came home the week she was away, and he and Rachel went for long walks. To Rachel's surprise and dismay, Daniel continued to regress with more secrets, telling her about his doubts about himself in bed, about some old friend from college, a woman who'd lived on his floor in the dorm, who called him pretty regularly. He said this with some bravado. Rachel was glad at least for that. But he was thinking of sleeping with that girl. How could that be the right thing to do? Rachel listened, said little, thought she should have been glad for the intimacy, but became alarmed by how much she knew about both her son and his wife.

Her dismay over all this led to the cake incident. The night before Daniel flew back to Seattle, after they'd had dinner and too much wine, Al and Rachel and Daniel took the top of the wedding cake Rachel had been keeping in the freezer in the basement since the wedding two years ago, took it into the backyard, and stomped on it. Rachel had brought the cake upstairs to the kitchen, where Al was refilling Daniel's glass with wine. The thin layer of ice crystals on the cardboard box melted, dripped down her wrists, making her feel chilled and weepy, just like the damned cake inside the box. She told Daniel, "Let's take it outside and smash it. It'll make us all feel better." So they did. They took it to the backyard and the three of them stomped on it. They were all three a little drunk, and at first it seemed to make some sort of sense.

For one thing, the three of them had a history of smashing things. When Daniel was sixteen, a junior, and a star member of the Lincoln-Douglas debate team, he'd been robbed of the chance to go to the National Tournament because the coach believed the choice should be made based on seniority. Daniel had held his trophy over his head outside the gymnasium, where he'd learned that the senior who'd come in second would represent the team. Rachel said, "Go ahead," surprising herself by her own desire to throw something. Daniel smashed the trophy into its glued sections: the statue, the base, the first prize plaque on the base—all separated rather neatly. Rachel picked up the little gold Abraham Lincoln—first prize was Lincoln; second, Douglas—held it over her head and waited. She was hardly violent; why, she'd never before broken anything on purpose. Daniel said to his mother, "Oh, go ahead," and she'd thrown it, watched the head break from the body, roll into the grass, seen the paint chip and fall like little gold stars, tiny emblems of all that Daniel had achieved, splattered on the sidewalk. Al picked the base up from the cement, handed it to Daniel, who said, "You do it, Dad." Al cracked the base in half and then collected all the pieces. Rachel put them in a shoe box labeled DEBATE, 1987 in the basement in a larger box near the freezer labeled DANIEL'S BOX. It sat next to the one labeled MIRIAM'S BOX. In these boxes Rachel saved mementos from her children's youth: their Mother's Day cards, all their report cards, early finger paintings, Miriam's first grade picture of a cutout butterfly pasted and floating on a background of scribbled chalk—sun, grass, house (right in the center)—on now-faded construction paper; Daniel's owl that he made when he was seven with a rug-hooking kit given to him by Rachel's father who, after he retired, made crude oriental-patterned rugs—no one liked them, but both Rachel and her mother displayed his rugs in their foyers.

After the cake incident, Rachel was horrified that she'd been oddly exhilarated by it—smashing the cake outside in the cold, their laughter. When Al asked Rachel, "How much was that cake, anyway?" the three of them turned into giggling, silly, drop-on-the-ground hysterics. The cake had been too old to be eaten, anyway—Daniel and Katya were in Seattle when their first anniversary passed. But Rachel later concluded it had been a bad idea. She became worried about her own behavior. One thing was certain: She was the one who'd brought the cake up from the basement.

She looked over at Martin, who sat across from her, waiting patiently for her to answer. *Who am I to accuse anyone?* she thought. *I need to get hold.* "I'll get the tea."

"I'll help."

"No, no."

But Martin was getting up. "Martin, please, this is all very difficult, somehow. I don't know. I just need to get the tea by myself. I'll be back." More than she could say for Martin Rubenstein.

"Rachel," said Martin, "are you sure you're all right?"

"Maybe you'd prefer coffee?"

"Yes," he said, "Coffee. Black, strong, please," and he sat back down, dropped into the chair. He looked as if his joints hurt, like an old man, tired, frustrated, his back and head bent. *Like my father*, Rachel thought, and moved quickly to the kitchen where the pie still sat ominously on the counter.

Rachel poured Martin a cup of steaming coffee. Thirty years and she'd never confronted him. She'd gone on, tried to forget it. Al had been there. Al was always there. The thought of Al, of his body next to hers after they made love in the morning, comforted her. But even that was tenuous—a gesture, the wave of his hand to stop her chatter while he was puzzling at breakfast over something on the business page in the *Sun*, would remind her of his life away from her at work, and then she would think that moment of sweet-smelling skin and locked eyes could not have really mattered.

And what about Daniel and Katya? One week after Katya ran off to Italy she'd come back with no remorse. But Daniel took her back. He admitted he'd been a terrible husband, not listening, falling asleep after work, too tired for sex. He'd reported on the phone that Katya said, "Well, now we're even. The playing field's been leveled."

Rachel was speechless. How could Katya think, let alone say, such a thing?

"No kidding," was all that Al, on the extension, said, filling in her silence. Later he reached across the kitchen table and covered Rachel's hand with his own to comfort her. She was bereft to see her son betrayed. "So," Al said when he took his hand away, "does this mean you'll continue being Katya's sounding board? Are you cured of that?" His hand went to that place atop his head. Did Al know that Rachel was aware of Katya's plans? Rachel felt more chastened than comforted.

Before Daniel hung up, Rachel finally managed to say something, but it was hardly adequate, "Falling asleep on the couch is not exactly immoral." How could the playing field be level when Katya betrayed Daniel? Maybe Rachel had betrayed her own son by accepting Katya's confidences, complaints. Oh, she felt useless, a mess of contradictions. She remembered something from the poem Katya asked her to read at the wedding: *I saw you everywhere*, something like that, *in the trees, in the stars*. It was trite, but nonetheless had moved Rachel with its certainty, and she had cried a bit while she'd read it. "I'm confused," she admitted, more to herself than to Daniel.

"That makes two of us," said Daniel.

"Three," Al said on the extension.

And here Rachel stood, more confused than ever, with Martin's cup of coffee still in her hand.

"Rachel," Martin said, taking the coffee from her, "please sit down. I want to talk to you."

The phone rang, which was fortunate timing but no coincidence; she looked at her watch and knew it would be Al.

Martin put his coffee on the side table and his head in his hands. He looked like a man who'd made a mistake and knew it.

"Al!" Rachel said brightening her voice, as if she'd never expected to hear from him.

"You're using your telephone voice on me. What's the matter?"

"Why, nothing, dear."

"That voice you use for repairmen, for department store clerks who annoy you."

"Al," Rachel's sing-song voice said, "really."

"Rachel. It's four. This is when I always call. What's wrong?"

"Yes, dear."

"Yes, dear?" He repeated her silliness.

She was paralyzed. Had she really thought Martin would be gone by now? Was that why she'd thought it unnecessary to tell Al this was the day he was coming? Why worry him? But she must have secretly known she might need Al. That, of course, was why she scheduled the visit at three. She turned her back to Martin and whispered into the phone, "I made a cherry pie."

Al laughed and then whispered back, "Well, I think it's done you in."

"No, no, I'm fine," Rachel whispered.

"But why are we whispering?" whispered Al.

"You know I love you," whispered Rachel.

"Yes, dear," said Al, and then, "Now you've got me doing it."

"Yes, dear," she said again.

"Rachel, go lie down. I'll be home at the usual time."

"Yes, dear," she repeated and put the phone in its cradle, feeling foolish and flighty and scared, thinking, cradle to grave, love and death. Why these words? Pulling herself together, she said, "Martin Rubenstein, it's time we talked."

When Rachel sat down and faced Martin, he had the letters, blue airmail onionskin envelopes with their thin red borders, in his hands. The letters were tied with a piece of string. He laid them on the side table and began to talk. He recalled the time he'd taken her sailing in his tiny Sunfish on the Maggothy River. She was sixteen, precocious, and already a freshman at the University of Maryland. He was in the U of M's dental school. While he talked, her mind drifted to the images from that time before he'd kissed her, before his father died. She remembered how their hands brushed when he pulled the sail to turn about, how with her head bent, she looked up into his face. She thought of all the years she'd done that, when she was smaller than he. She remembered how tongue-tied she'd been the whole trip, how she always feared speaking to him, how her shyness, the shyness that had plagued her since she was little, worsened in his presence.

"You were yare," he said.

Why, he's quoting movie dialogue. *The Philadelphia Story*. Cary Grant to Katherine Hepburn when Hepburn talks longingly of the yacht she and Grant had owned, and Grant then rekindles lost love with shared memory. Rachel knew the movie well. Why would Martin choose this movie dialogue—did he know it was one of her favorites? He couldn't possibly. They'd never even watched a movie together. "Love gone wrong," she said, "then right."

"I've come long after I should have."

Martin was looking way too comfortable in the wing chair. After dinner, this was where she and Al put their feet up, talked and read their books, side by side, each with a crook-neck halogen lamp for good, solid light. She said to Martin, "Late, you might say?" with a question in her voice that she answered by deciding she'd never tell him the chair's secret.

He put both his hands on the letters. "You might not even want to listen."

He was guarding the letters, that's what he was doing, as if they were damn crown jewels. She said, "Funny, but I don't think I want to read them—I'd thought I would, but now I think I would see how foolish I was—am."

"I was the fool."

So, finally she was to hear the explanation. "The silent fool?" she said with an edge in her voice that she regretted as the words registered on Martin's mournful face. She said, "You didn't cry at the funeral." It was an odd thing to say, as if she was changing the subject. But his reaction, his lugubrious face told her it was the subject, somehow.

"I went back to Alaska. I didn't cry there either. I read all your letters. It was a good place to be depressed. No sun, the night that lasts round the clock. You wrote beautiful letters, about the books you were reading, about Thoreau and E. M. Forster. I've reread those letters, thought about you quoting to me, about being awake to life, about the things that won't forsake us. About connecting, paying attention to the details, thinking of life as one critical hour. I can't quote it for you, but you remember— and then the letters asking me why I didn't write."

Now would be the time for Rachel to finally ask him "Why?" But her head was full of details, piling in, one on the other, confusing her. And Martin's words, Thoreau's words, "the critical hour," made her think about her father—she wished Al were here to get her out of this muddle. But here she sat with Martin, alone, the way she'd planned it. She said, "And then we just went on, didn't we? Never talking about it. I think your mother and my parents were relieved it was over. Cousins marrying!"

"So somehow we put it away like a dirty little secret. You never asking me. Me never willing to talk about it. And then you married Al."

"And then I married Al. Now that explains everything, doesn't it?" Rachel was annoyed. Maybe she didn't want to hear Martin's belated explanation. She said, "Did you know, Martin, that Celia's ninety-three-year-old mother won't speak to her? Why, she's banned Celia from the nursing home."

"Rachel, I'm trying to explain."

"No listen. Don't you want to know why?"

"Well, yes, of course, but—"

"Martin, I know I've behaved like a silly schoolgirl. That's the way I've always behaved around you. But listen, this will help. Celia's mother doesn't speak to her and Celia is seventy-five years old. She doesn't speak to her, she says, because Celia, a Catholic, married a Jew—my sweet, old, Jewish father."

"But Rachel, what's this got to do with us?"

There was no "us" between Martin and Rachel. She thought about saying so, but she asked instead, "Well, how is that to be understood?" referring to Celia and her ninety-three-year-old mother. "The woman is seventy-five years old, for God's sake.

Not everything makes sense. Contradictions. They're everywhere. Martin, maybe you don't need to explain."

"Of course I do."

"Martin, you know what?" Rachel stood up, smoothed her hair. "It's too late." She was still mad at him, at the self-important way he'd kept his hands on her love letters. Why, he'd betrayed her by not answering them—well, not exactly the way Katya had betrayed Daniel, but it was unforgivable, wasn't it? To have left her in the dark, to have professed his love, to have kissed her with such tenderness and passion, to have asked her to marry him, and then just left—gone away? The way he hadn't written. For six months she'd written, every day at first, then once a week until finally she'd given up. She felt like smashing something just thinking about it. That would be a nice little headline for Martin to take home with him: "Crazy cousin strikes aging dentist with cherry pie."

She smiled thinking about it and then realized she was not about to smash anything with Martin around; she didn't know him well enough. She could smash things around Daniel and Miriam and Al. They would go on doing crazy things. She smiled thinking about Miriam giggling, saying, "Mom, tell me." She thought of Daniel and the cake. Yes, they have a history of smashing things. You bet they do. It's history they've got. Rachel wanted to see Al. She wanted Martin to leave. Martin couldn't possibly understand. Feed him and get rid of him. That's what she'd do.

She said, "How about a piece of pie?"

But Martin was slow to leave. Once he'd eaten the pie and praised the crust, he kept fiddling with his fork, asking for more coffee. But, thank goodness, he'd given up trying to talk to her about the love letters, about the past.

Finally she got him into the foyer, near the door, but he wasn't budging. She thought he'd never leave. No matter. She knew where she belonged and why. She was a little anxious that Al would walk in on them. It was late, almost time. That was bothering her. But why should it? They were just old cousins having a visit.

"Martin, it's been good seeing you." She extended her hand. "After all these years." She felt silly saying that, reaching out to shake his hand like an old acquaintance—for he was hardly that, and she knew it. He was a man she'd almost married.

Martin took her hand and, with a courtly bow, bent and kissed it. And with that curve still in his back, he looked up to meet her eyes. "You were my missed chance. That's what I came to tell you."

She considered pulling her hand away but couldn't because that's what she'd been waiting to hear, wasn't it? That she was the one he'd loved all these years. But he hardly knew her. Thirty years and they'd barely spoken at family get-togethers. This wasn't about love. She didn't know what it was about, but she knew it wasn't love. She said, "No, that's not it, Martin. You're just getting old and worrying about dying." She was being flip, trying to get him out the door, maybe even wanting to hurt his ego now that she had the upper hand.

But Martin stood there, holding her hand, silent. He finally said, "I never told my father I loved him, Rachel. Did I ever tell you that? I couldn't say it. He would tell me, even when I was grown, he would tell me, surprise me with it. But I couldn't get the words out of my mouth. What an arrogant, hard-ass I was. It's unforgivable, isn't it?" And he started to cry. Her old cousin, her old friend, crying in her foyer.

She took him in her arms, patting him on the shoulder the way she'd done to comfort Miriam and Daniel when they were little, when they were hurt. "Martin, I wasn't your missed chance.

I was just there and Abe wasn't." That was it, wasn't it? All her annoyance at the letters that he'd never answered dissipated. She finally understood. "Martin, he'd left you, and I was there, an old friend, a cousin who loved him. You know how much I loved Abe?"

Martin wept into Rachel's shoulder. He didn't say anything.

"Martin, Abe was the one who gave me the first stamps for my album. Do you remember how he used to save them up until my mother and father brought me over for a visit? And when he was dying, when he lay there in the den on the old couch, and I would come? It was so hard to look at him—he was so thin. He was all teeth. And he would smile at me."

Martin stood back, held Rachel by her shoulders. "The only one," he said, "who could make him smile."

When Rachel looked at him as if he were giving her another unearned compliment, he said, "That's what my mother told me when I got home to visit him that last time before he died."

Rachel held Martin close again and thought about her own father whom she'd told many times how much she loved him, who had told her more and more these days and who, despite Celia's boasting of his sexual prowess, was frustrated with living. He was able to do less and less for himself. Celia was helping him with his jacket, to get it on and off, not as she first had—because of her South American upbringing—but because he couldn't do it himself. On Rachel's last visit, as she'd shut the door behind her, she'd heard Celia say, "Sam, I'll give you your bath now." Rachel concluded that her father couldn't bathe himself anymore, that Celia must help him dress too.

With Martin's head on her shoulder, she thought: *When my father dies, both my parents will be gone, and I'll be left, waiting my turn, waiting for all the ways that life betrays the living with its wearing down and wearing out.* That's what Rachel thought, holding Martin in her arms.

And that's when Al turned the key in the door.

"Al, you remember Martin?" Rachel wiped tears from her face with the Kleenex she had in her apron pocket. Then she handed the tissue to Martin, and her eyes followed Al's, following the intimate gesture of a shared hanky.

Martin was finally ready to leave. "I've really got to get going." He shook Al's hand vigorously.

Martin hadn't changed. He was abandoning her again. But she smiled, because that was not really so. This time she would be all right.

With Martin out the door, Al walked past her to the kitchen, where she found him studying the pie on the counter. "So you two started without me," he said into the pie plate, his back to her. Yes, she heard the irony, the one-liner, more kind than she deserved.

She came up behind him, put her arms around him. "I should have told you he was coming. I know I should have." And she meant it.

"Umm," Al turned to look at her. He looked and waited.

"I almost married him, you know."

Al knew that. He knew her better than anybody. When she stated the obvious, he had always laughed. He looked at her now. And she watched him closely—not even a smile.

"Remember the peach pie?" she said. When she was pregnant with Daniel, she'd made a peach pie in the morning and all day long, after each household task, rewarded herself with a piece of the pie until only the empty pie plate was left when Al got home. A thin woman, she'd been ravenous when pregnant. Al loved repeating the story to the children.

"How could I forget? I never got any of that one."

"Well, this pie should have been all yours like that one."

"No, that pie went in the right place, to the right stomachs. Now, this one—"

Her arms around Al's waist, she could smell the last of his aftershave mixed with the smell of his skin, the odor that she yearned for when she leaned against his back at night.

She said, "You make my heart beat."

He turned to face her, leaned back, placed his hands on her shoulders. "You've got a lot of explaining to do. You know that, don't you?" But he smiled.

"Oh, how about a piece of pie?" she said. "And then I'll tell you everything." Al used to make her crazy eating dessert before dinner. He'd come home from work when the kids were little, and Al and Miriam and Daniel would sit at the kitchen table, right in front of her, eating chocolate chip cookies that Rachel had baked, eating them before dinner while Rachel shouted at them, "I've got my mother's brisket in the oven. It took me all day to make it." They'd smile sheepishly at each other and then run around Rachel, shoving cookies at her. She thought now of her own mother standing in front of her white porcelain counter with brisket in butcher paper, the onions still in their skins, the carrots yet to be scraped, the cans of Rokeach tomato sauce unopened.

"Everything?" The man of one-word sentences.

"Everything," and she kissed him on the mouth, knowing she would never again think of Martin's kiss the way she used to.

She put her hands around Al's face, this face she knew so well. His solid presence, her day with Martin, made her wonder if she would ever understand all the contradictions. They kept coming, tossed into her life. Like dreams—that came from nowhere in her sleep and made no sense when she awoke.

"Let's go into the living room," he said, "put some music on."

Perhaps a turn around the rug? "And then," she said, "we'll eat the pie together." She thought of all the times they'd made love, how, when they were done, she'd lain inside his arms, warm and vulnerable and safe. She ached inside for him—and for her father who was bent and frail, whose whole body curved like a thin hand in a wave of farewell. *Fare well*—she said the words in her head. But how to find the way?

And yet, Al—seeing him, touching his head, lying against him when they slept—gave her comfort. Though she wasn't sure exactly how she'd explain all that had happened to her that afternoon, she knew he'd understand the way she knew his voice.

He nuzzled in her neck. "Dessert first, huh?"

"Well, we're married, aren't we?"

And then he laughed. That laugh—the simple, truthful sound of him.

Trouble with Kitchens

It all started again, Eliot's problems with kitchens, after she met the doctor, the orthopedist who was going to fix her knee. He was so tall, so self-assured, so awfully good-looking in that way that athletes exude good health and certainty.

Aren't all orthopedists former jocks with brains, but without that perfect timing to have made it to the pros—as in hit or catch or throw the ball at the ineffable moment that defines glory? That was her theory, anyway.

On the second visit, after the MRI, after he'd told her she had a torn cartilage and that he could do something—"Noninvasive, a little scoping, that's all"—after he started sneezing and then coughing, when she said, "Are you all right?" and he shook his head, yes, still coughing, and she offered him the bottle of Evian in the outside pocket of her backpack, said, "I haven't opened it yet," and he shook his head, no, and managed to say, "Just hay fever," and she said, "You know, they have a lot of good drugs for that," and he barely managed to say, "I know," when she said, "But you didn't take yours this morning, did you?" and he shook his head, no, and began laughing while he was coughing and sniffling, she knew her kitchen was in trouble.

She was already in trouble because she didn't think her

husband, Max, had been telling her the truth lately. She knew about this sort of thing. She'd been married before. She knew what men could do after they'd been married a while, when a new kitchen was about to be. She knew.

She stood now in her completely gutted kitchen and tried to imagine the 48-inch Viking stove, the big-chested Sub-Zero refrigerator, the new granite island, all on order. But it was hard, even though the sink with the disposal Max had had to kick to get going was gone. The first time he'd put down his tools and tried the all-purpose, fix-the-juke-box, get-the-candy-or-cigarettes-to-fall-to-the-vending-machine-slot kick, both the disposal and the stove came on. The stove that seemed to have a mind of its own—"Today I'm on; let ya know about tomorrow"—was also gone. The refrigerator and the wall behind it that stood oddly in the center of the room and blocked the sun from the breakfast room windows—Who on earth had come up with that silly design?—gone. All the walls stripped. The room, which had no heat—which had been so cold this past winter that she'd come down to make coffee one morning, opened the cupboard to get the paper filter and saw solid white peanut and olive oil on the shelf above the coffee beans—was now hot. No air-conditioning either. She was in an empty room. Empty is what she saw. No kitchen is what she saw. Gone is what she saw.

After all, she had experience losing kitchens. She'd lost two: one for Max and one for the move to this quirky old three-story brownstone.

She liked that word *brownstone*, as if she lived in Manhattan in some artsy neighborhood. But it was a narrow row house like the one she'd grown up in. Only this one had one more story. So in that sense she'd taken a step up. And these weren't ordinary stories. The ceilings were twelve feet high. That's a lot of steps from one story to another, and that was part of her problem. Going up and down all those stairs, dropping that box on her knee during the move, had brought her to the tall orthopedist in the first place. But in the second place, on that second visit, he'd helped her figure out what she might do.

So, in the middle of her kitchen's about-to-be that she couldn't conjure up, she decided what she'd say to Tony Unger before they went into the operating room together. He'd begin, "Ms. Bernstein"—he didn't say "Mrs." the first time or the second time they met, and she'd found this au courant, if not downright seductive. She knew you had to listen carefully for hidden cues, the subtle hints of something about to happen. So, when he'd say, "Ms. Bernstein, do you have any questions?" she'd interrupt and say, "You're about to slice open my knee, don't you think we should be on a first-name basis?" and take her first step toward giving up her kitchen.

She knew it would soon be history because she had more than suspicions about Max. She had data.

The other day, she'd been complaining about ridges in her fingernail, the one that she'd broken while carrying the box she'd dropped on her knee. And he'd said, "I hear that comes from smoking. You been smoking?" He knew she'd stopped years ago.

"Who told you that?"

"That you'd been sneaking smokes?"

Actually, she'd had one or two illicit cigarettes when he wasn't around, when she was out for a drink with her one girl-friend who smoked. How did he know this? "No, about ridges."

"I don't remember," he said.

Ah, the tip off. *I don't remember.* That's what the guilty guy always says when he might incriminate himself on the stand. She'd seen Perry Mason cut through to the truth enough times to know he was dissembling. Now it was her turn. "That's the kind of conversation you'd have with a woman. Men don't talk about their nails. Who was she?"

"Eliot, what are you talking about?" He didn't even wait for an answer. He started reading the paper. Avoiding her, no doubt.

But that wasn't all. There was something worse. There was that makeup mirror she'd found in his travel pack when they went to Florida to visit his parents. It was small with a powder-blue plastic edge, and lying right next to it was liquid concealer. Max was having an affair. She knew it.

On the day of the surgery at Sibley Hospital in D.C., not far from the old house with the empty kitchen and the three stories, Tony didn't say much at all.

With Max sitting next to her, she met André, the anesthesiologist, who was not as tall as Tony but had a fine head of black, straight hair and an Eastern European last name and accent. Romania? Bulgaria? Transylvania—even better, she thought, remembering what Bram Stoker called "the center of some sort of imaginative whirlpool." But when André rolled an R with the question, "Rough time with your knee, huh?" she thought Czechoslovakia, sure of it because her carpenter, a precise young man with tools she couldn't name, rolled his Rs exactly that way.

Radovan with his hand on his tool belt, saying, "We're going to have to take that wall down. It's rrrotten," had rolled his Rs right into her heart. Every day he came, suggested a change that did result in that awful word from the main office, *Upcharge*, as in "Sure, we'll do it, but that'll be an upcharge," he created firm ground, a living force against decay, the damage of termites and old age. He repaired. Her kitchen walls would be strong, her appliances would fit perfectly, and that retractable step under the island, the one he'd designed and was building to raise her up to give her the leverage she'd need to bake bread, would be solid because Radovan kept making small adjustments to refine the architect's kitchen plans. Nate, the architect, would stand by, rub his head and say, "I guess we do need to do that." Radovan made her feel safe.

His rolled *R*s rubbed off on André and she knew she'd be okay. She said to André, "Bungee jumping. Gotta cut it out."

He laughed. She liked him for that. She was nearly fifty though she didn't look it, weighed the same she'd weighed when she'd married the guy before Max, the one who still had her first kitchen. But time does take its toll, and she was sitting there with nothing on but a short hospital gown that revealed that crinkly skin above her knees. When had that happened?

She and André were looking at her knee when Tony walked in and said, not "Ms. Bernstein, do you have any questions?" but "Someone should have marked that knee." No, hello, no intro to Max, no questions. He pulled a pen from his sports jacket—he wasn't even wearing those crisp, loose-fitting, turquoise operating pajamas that André had on and that revealed André's nicely defined upper biceps. When was Tony going to change? Weren't they going together into the operating room? She'd imagined him holding her hand as her gurney was wheeled down the hallway. She imagined seeing Tony's biceps, because she knew orthopedists had to be strong to wield those big drills, make holes in bones, realign spinal columns, make right what time had worn out. That was why they were tall and, almost all of them, men. They needed the leverage of height the way she needed to be raised up above her island to put the force of her weight on bread dough and make it come alive. Tony marked her knee with two *X*s and a circle, and André asked her to open her mouth.

"I've just had my teeth cleaned," she said. She'd been to the dentist last week, learned that a gold inlay was in need of repair. Was there no end to the retooling, the needed renewals? She felt like a magazine subscription, running out.

Again he laughed and rolled his R. "*Rrroom* enough. You're fine."

"Room enough for what?" She was going in for a knee operation. What did her mouth have to do with this?

"You'll be asleep," André said. "I'll be putting something in your mouth to make sure you don't gag on your tongue."

She might gag? Her mouth dropped open.

"Standard procedure. Not anything to worry about." *Worrrrry,* he said. *Prrrrocedure.* "Now let's have a look at those veins."

"Don't put the IV in my hand," she said. "I have tiny veins, but they're there. I'm alive, aren't I? Go for the arm where it won't hurt." She'd had blood taken many times for routine tests and physicals and knew that the bruise on the hand hurt a lot worse than being stuck more than once while an inexperienced technician probed around inside the crook of her elbow.

"I've already looked at those tiny wrists. I know what I'm up against," André said, and followed with a series of horrifying questions about heart palpitations, drug allergies, and breathing disorders, which she answered in the negative, and then he said, "But what's this 'Gimme a break?' on your release form?" That was what she'd written on the form to counter the legal boilerplate that said, to her disbelief: "Standard operating procedure may include misplacement of anesthesia."

"Standard legal jargon," she said, referring to her bracketed note. "You're asking me to give you permission to misplace the anesthesia? Is that standard operating procedure? Where you gonna put it? In my ear instead of my arm?" Was this a release for incompetence?

"Don't worry," André repeated and held her hand while he looked at her veins.

Tony said, "See you soon." They both left her alone with Max, who had sat mute through all the exchanges. He was reading the business page of the *Washington Post.* Was everyone unaware of the apparent danger here?

In the operating room, Tony was nowhere in sight, although she'd seen him standing in the hall on her way and had sat up and said, "Tony, why am I on a stretcher? I want to go dancing." He waved, laughed, still in his sports jacket standing with a younger and quite handsome guy by his side. That guy was wearing those hospital fatigues Tony should have had on. Was he going to do the operation? Was there a secret switch here in the works? Tony said, "You will, you will."

André put the IV in her hand, saying, "I like to listen to the patient, but in this case ..."; she was thinking, going, going, gone—like my kitchen—and fell asleep.

No one dreams under general anesthesia. Out cold. But if she had dreamed, she would have dreamed of Max and the man on the number five bus and when she'd had to decide which one of them she loved more. That was after she'd left her first brand new kitchen—before the electrician had hooked up the new GE oven, built-in microwave under the hood—*and* her first husband. He'd been having an affair with his secretary, Mary, for over a year.

She would have dreamed of the night he'd danced with Mary at the Christmas party, right in front of her, dance after dance while she sat alone with his coworkers with nothing to say. This was after he'd told her about the affair, confessed it because "You're my best friend. Who else can I tell?" This was after he'd also told her "It's over. I love *you*." But there he was, dancing with Mary.

So on the Monday after the Christmas party, she went to work and told Max, her coworker, about it at lunch. She asked Max to lunch. He'd never talked much to her before, seemed surprised by the invitation, but suggested a quiet place, a long walk from their office.

She was not attracted to Max, but he was steady, reliable, good-natured, and had once told her that he'd been divorced. "A long time ago, part of my history," he'd said. "Not important," he'd said. She couldn't recall how any of that had come up. But he was divorced. Maybe he could help because she was thinking about leaving this man she'd called her husband for the last ten years and who now seemed like anything but. She couldn't even say his name out loud anymore. He'd become a nameless fixture in her life and in the house he'd built for them with a big wide kitchen, almost finished, with brand new fixtures for everything, many of which she also couldn't name. She'd picked out knobs and buttons and switches and faucets, all with names and order numbers that had to be remembered or who knows what would have happened?

That new house was like none she'd ever seen or ever hoped for. In the kitchen, the trash can was hidden behind a cabinet and conveniently tipped forward when she pulled on the door. She had a hidden ironing board. Not that that had much to do with cooking, but the laundry room was right off the mudroom, off the kitchen, near the back stairway. A back stairway! That new kitchen had a fireplace, too, and the all-important suburban deck.

She'd grown up in a Baltimore row house with stairs to the second floor and stairs to the basement and a view from the front door to the back door and the clothes tree outside the door. Her childhood house didn't have hallways or a foyer. There was no place to hide anything or to hide. She could hear the neighbors when they argued and everything that everyone said inside her narrow house was fair game for anyone in the back, the front, up or down the stairs.

She told Max at lunch, "He'd been hiding this. I didn't see anything, know anything. I've been a dunce."

"No," Max said, "you weren't looking because you didn't think you needed to," and he handed her a bread stick. Their hands brushed. He ordered her a glass of wine.

She said, "We have to go back to work."

He said, "Eliot," just her name, as if he were hearing it for the first time, saying it out loud to remember it. She heard her name, and then quiet. He was looking at her. Simply looking. She looked back. She noticed that his eyes were deep and dark but blue. Night blue, the color of the sky when it's time to sleep, to rest. She began to have lunch with him every day. He did the asking then, and at every lunch, she rested from the turmoil at home, the arguments, the negotiations about who would get what. "I won't take anything," she'd finally said, and started looking for an apartment far from her dream house, closer to work. She began riding the number five bus. At lunch, she listened to Max say her name the way no one else had ever said it. Each time he said her name, he stopped and looked at her. Each time, she heard something new.

Over hamburgers and French fries, "Eliot, how are you deep down inside?"

"I don't know. You?"

"Confused," he'd said. "Now you."

She was confused. She'd met the man on the number five bus by then. "Deep down inside, I'm from Baltimore."

And he'd laughed. She didn't think she was funny. No one before had laughed at her odd, slightly off-base humor.

While eating pizza with pepperoni, "Eliot," while he looked down at his plate and his voice dropped as if he'd been hurt. She'd said something about the man on the number five bus.

And then one day, after his last swallow of hot and sour soup, "Eliot," and she could see in his night-blue eyes a real live boyish tear that actually slipped out onto his ruddy cheek. She watched it cling to the bit of stubble high on his cheekbone that he must have missed shaving that morning. She was transfixed by that tiny drop, watched it dry. He didn't reach up to pat it the way she would have. He ignored it as if it hadn't happened. It could've been the Great Wall's loose hand with hot pepper. They were noted for their fiery Szechuan dishes that could make any grown man cry. But she had just said she was going on a date with the man on the bus. She'd never forget that tear. It must have blurred his vision for a brief second. He wore contact lenses, she learned later, when he cried watching Clint Eastwood standing in the rain in *The Bridges of Madison County*, a chick-flick if there ever was one, and he'd had to take his lenses out. She knew Max had been sad that day at lunch and she'd done it, not understanding that Max was in love. Max said, "Eliot, have dinner with me." And she did.

But first she had lunch at La Brazzerie on Capitol Hill with the man on the number five bus. She'd been looking at him for weeks and didn't know if he'd been looking at her because it seemed that everyone was looking at her when she dragged her three bags onto the bus each morning—her briefcase, her purse, her gym bag—and invariably dropped one of them. One morning, he retrieved her purse, handed it to her. And she met his eyes, so brown, so intense that in that brief moment of eye contact she felt as if she were traveling so fast she might die. She'd heard that if you could travel at the speed of light, you'd become light itself. Like matter changing into energy. She could barely look at him.

One day, standing at the subway after the bus ride, he'd spoken to her, and somehow she'd given him her first name and apparently enough information to find her at her job, because that's exactly what he did. First he sent her those branches of weeping cherry, pink and delicate, lying in tissue paper, and believe it or not, signed, "For Eliot, who defies logic. From the guy on the number five bus." Then he called and asked her to lunch. She was seduced by the force of his effort.

At lunch, she had even more trouble looking at him, trouble not touching his long thin fingers, the silver rope bracelet on his wrist. She did slip one finger beneath the bracelet on parting, and to her horror nearly swooned like an ingenue in a Victorian novel. She now knew that his name was Timothy.

Later, after she'd slept with him at lunchtime at the Tabard Inn on N street, against her better judgment and with an unrestrained excitement she'd never known and would never know again, she also learned that he was married.

And that's when she had dinner with Max.

She would have dreamed all this because kitchens and men and new men and old ones and getting old and needing repair and Viking stoves and big-chested refrigerators are all about love, despite what your stomach tells you. She knew this the way she knew that her kitchen was going, going, gone because she knew that Max didn't love her anymore. She was sure of it.

Eliot woke with a bang on the head. She saw Max and then André, and a young strawberry blond-haired nurse said, "Sorry, but I caught it before—"

André interrupted, "Before we'd need stitches."

What were they talking about? Max had her hand now, and she saw the nurse hang a plastic bag of some sort of fluid on a metal pole. Her head was fuzzy and she had a headache. "Am I okay?"

"You're fine," said André, "except that we did hit you in the head."

"Why?" She'd lost her sense of humor. She wanted to see her leg. Was she bleeding? Why did she need an IV?

"It wasn't on purpose," said the nurse. "The IV pole slipped, but I caught it. Are you okay?"

How was she supposed to know?

"How about some water or cranberry juice?" said the nurse.

"Could I have tea?" and that's when the shivering started. She was so cold she was shaking all over. "I'm not okay, am I?" She looked at Max. He looked concerned. "Tell me," she said. "What happened? Where's Tony?" She wanted Tony to put his big warm hands around her the way he did when he held her knee the first time she'd met him. She wanted warm. Max's hand was cold. He must be nervous, she thought. I'm in trouble, she thought.

"Oh, he's cleaning up," said André. "The shivering is normal after anesthesia, especially when you haven't got all that much fat. It's cold in the operating room. Everything went swell," and he was gone, saying to the nurse, "Get her some tea."

Max said, "The doctor spoke with me. Said it all went as planned."

The nurse wrapped her in blankets, even around her head, gave her some tea. She warmed up quickly and looked at the gigantic ace bandage that started at the top of her thigh and ended at her ankle. She was sure she was dying.

And then another nurse appeared and said, "Okay, let's see if you can stand up, if you need help dressing."

She stood up with Max on one side and the nurse on the other. "Okay?" asked the new nurse. "I'm letting go. You're in his hands." Eliot leaned toward Max. "She'll be fine, but yell if you need anything. As soon as she's dressed, I'll get someone to wheel her downstairs."

"A wheelchair? Why do I need that?"

"You don't really," said the nurse, well on her way to the next patient, calling over her shoulder, "we wheel everybody out. No exceptions."

In the car, Eliot said to Max again, "Tell me the truth."

"Eliot, I did. You've got a prescription for Percocet. I'll take you home and then get it filled. The only other thing he said was that he also used a local on the knee, so you won't feel much pain until that wears off, but you should probably take a pill before then. Try to head it off. Eliot, you're fine."

And she was. She knew she was. But what was she supposed to do about Max?

Two days later, she went to see Tony to have the ace bandage removed. Max drove her, took the morning off to do it. She'd said, "I can take a cab. You're busy."

He'd said, "Eliot, look at you."

He used to say that whenever he met her for dinner before they got married, before they bought this tall skinny house with its impossible stairs that she now couldn't climb. She was stuck on the second floor. He'd brought her her laptop so she could get e-mail from the office. He'd brought her Cup-a-Soup that he'd heated up in the microwave that was also in the bedroom. Their kitchen had walls now, it had cabinets, it had plumbers, it had Radovan with his tool belt, now laying new wood flooring. But still they couldn't cook. Still the kitchen was to be—the way she and Max once were. Not the way they were now: finished like a story that's over and not worth reading again.

Max used to say "Eliot, look at you," and she'd hear in his voice, in the way his words came slow, as if that was all he had to do or could do, look, she'd hear summer. A February storm could be blowing outside, and with his words she'd see herself through the haze of a screen door that wouldn't shut. She'd hear it bang and see the open space that no one bothers to close. She'd see herself wearing a long cotton skirt, a white camisole loose across her bare breasts, what one wears on humid, breezy, open afternoons.

Now she heard, "Eliot, look at you," and knew she was old and broken and used. Why would he want her? He didn't want her. She knew it. She longed for Tony's warm hands on that knee that hurt so much she felt as if she were storing steel wool—the steel wool she would use to clean the Viking's giant drip pan under the brand-new six burners—steel wool, smack in the center of her joint. Tony would put his hands on her knee and tell her it would be all right.

But Tony was on vacation, and when she said to Dr. Lewis, "Why does it hurt so much?" he said, "I wasn't the attending physician." She couldn't believe it. He must be telling her this because the news was so bad. He said, "Do fifty leg lifts a day. Here's a prescription for Tylenol 3. Take it easy, now," and he was gone, white coat flying behind him. He was out the door so quickly she couldn't ask him even one more question.

When Max saw her, he said, "Eliot, Eliot, what's wrong?"

She was crying. "I don't know. I guess I hurt."

He had his arm around her now. "Let's get you home. Oh, Eliot."

There he was again saying her name. This time she heard her mother. When she was little, had strep throat, couldn't talk, her mother made homemade chicken soup. Max said, "Oh, Eliot," and she could see the sliced carrots floating among the parsley her mother had chopped to garnish the soup, the tender pieces of chicken she'd simmered for hours sliding around the edges of her best china. Her mother, who laid a delicate bowl on that old metal TV table with the painted flowers. Eliot could see the sun from the window through the bowl's edge because the china was so fine, only used for guests. Her mother, who sat down on the bed and pressed Eliot to her heavy bosom. And her mother's apron, fragrant with onions and garlic and soap, washed so many times it was soft like Max's old T-shirts that he wore to bed. Her mother, who'd died so many years ago. Now she heard her mother in the way Max said her name, and she laid her head on his chest. She didn't trust him, but who else would ever say her name that way?

So, she said, "Nice pecs," and wiped her nose on his shirt, the shirt he was going to wear to work after he dropped her off. "Oh, sorry," she said, patting the damp spot on his crisp blue shirt.

"It's drip dry," he said, and then surprised her by reaching one arm around her back and rubbing the side of her breast. "Yours too," he said, and took her home.

She was up and around the following week, and she had an appointment with Tony, finally back from vacation, on the same day that the Viking stove was going to be delivered. Radovan had assured her he'd be there if she didn't make it back in time. She might be late. This visit to Tony could take awhile. They'd have so much to discuss.

Tony did hold her knee in his big warm hand. He did look straight into her eyes, with big brown eyes that reminded her of Timothy, her wild affair, love in an inn with a married man. She looked at Tony's gold wedding band and waited to be seduced. He said, "Eliot," and then took the bad knee and flexed the joint, then the good one. "Take aspirin. Big Bear."

"Big Bear?" What was he talking about? Smoky the Bear, the three bears. She thought of sneaking cigarettes and Max finding out, about a ménage à trois: Max and her and that woman with the blue-rimmed makeup mirror. She wanted to seduce Tony, smoke in bed with him after sex, have her own triad. It was about time.

"It's a cheap brand. Aspirin, the miracle drug. And I'm giving you four weeks of physical therapy, and four more after that if you need it. Call Regional Rehab. Make an appointment, right now. You're doing great. Come back in two weeks."

She had no idea how to seduce anyone.

She went home disconsolate and achy, and at the Rite Aide near her house bought Bayer aspirin—she decided she deserved the best—and walked up her street to find her partially uncrated Viking stove on the asphalt and twenty-nine year-old Radovan chasing the delivery truck, shouting in Czech. The truck was rolling slowly, driverless, down the hill. Two workmen, one with a dolly, the other by her stove, were looking aghast at their truck and the disaster about to be. Radovan looped his six-foot-six frame onto the truck's open door, the truck stopped, and she knew she was in love with *him*.

That night when Max came home, she decided to confess. "I'm in love with Radovan." She felt foolish when she blurted this out. She barely knew him and was old enough to be his mother. She should have said, I'm an old fool. Why should you love me?

"Yeah, he's great, isn't he?" said Max. "The kitchen's going to be amazing." And with one hand he pushed open the door from the dining room, surveyed what Radovan had done today the way he did every night when he got home from work. With his other hand he swung a big brown bag of groceries onto the brand-new granite island.

Eliot followed him and stood before her new Viking stove. Radovan had helped the delivery guys get it in the house and then spent the rest of the day setting it in place. It was ready. She could cook if she wanted to. And Max had gone shopping. She pulled out of his bag the baguette that stuck out of the top.

But she wasn't thinking about food. She was thinking, *Why, he doesn't even think I could be in love with someone else.* She knew she was silly, but surely he knew she could wander? And then, apparently not. So she said, "No, no, you don't understand."

"Understand what?" He put his hands on the Viking knobs. These knobs were so big a man's hand looked good on them. She noticed that Max's hand, his solid fingers with their squared-off clean pared nails, the hands of a man who fixes things, fit on the big black knobs. His hands made her think about that other man, the one on the number five bus. Timothy. She recalled how she'd focused on his hands, those long slender fingers, because when she'd looked into his eyes, she'd been in danger, she'd been excited.

Max left the kitchen and came back with one of Eliot's copper pans. Everything was stored on the floor in the dining room. A mess of china and pots and pans collected over years of marriage and cooking lay out of place there. When he returned, he laid the pan on the brand-new burner and said, "How's your knee, Eliot?" He began emptying the grocery bag. Olive oil, garlic, plum tomatoes. He turned the burner on the stove and the flame shot blue-hot, like none she'd ever seen. "You were right," he said. "These open burners work." He was referring to her research on the stove. She'd learned that by not enclosing the burner, by using a big and difficult to clean drip pan underneath instead, more air could circulate and create a hotter flame.

"What's that got to do with anything?"

"Eliot, you've finally got your kitchen back. The one you lost, the one you wanted." He held up the loaf of French bread. "Have you tried out the step?" He was referring to Radovan's built-in under the island.

"Right, leverage." And of course that was what she needed, a way to get the edge on Max, get him to tell her the truth. She was going to get to the bottom of this. "Remember that time you cried at *The Bridges of Madison County*? Men don't cry at movies like that. And you did. I did think, oh golly, finally a sensitive guy. But now I think I should've asked."

"Asked what?"

"Who is she?"

"Who? Eliot, Eliot."

And this time she heard a screen door open somewhere. She could see another woman in a camisole, breathless from the heat, from his kiss. A redhead, freckles on translucent skin. Did he see her, too? In a haze of summer heat. Did a breeze blow in? Did the door slam? Did the woman turn away? Or did he?

"The other woman. That's who."

He laughed. "What other woman? Eliot, I thought you stopped taking the Percocet. Are you all right?"

This was no laughing matter. He could lose her and he should know it. "I could have chosen him. You know that, don't you?" This wasn't really so. A bit of a lie that Eliot told Max to make him see how serious she was. Timothy had, in the end, rejected Eliot. She'd never understood and sometimes wondered, hoped? if he'd done it because he loved her—to save her from the pain of an affair with a married man.

Max began emptying the grocery bag again. A box of DiCecco linguine appeared. "Choose who?" he asked. "Oh yeah, Radovan. Choose Radovan for what?"

Maybe she should call Timothy. She hadn't ever thought of doing that before. She could do that. Maybe she would. She was thrilled by a triad to be, love with a married man. But that line in *Dracula*, Stoker quoting Byron, came to mind, though she could never place the quote in any Byron poem that she knew: *And prove the truth he most abhorred*—and knew she'd never call him because she couldn't bear to know he'd slept with her and not wanted her again, that she'd just been one of many. Oh, what was she thinking? That silly gothic story that swirled inside her head. Women swept away. Was that what she wanted? To be swept off by Tony, André, Radovan? "Radovan?" she said. "No, of course not. The other guy. The one I was dating when I married you."

"Eliot." That's all he said and stopped emptying groceries, left his bag alone. He stood and looked at her. "Eliot." Again, her name.

She had his attention now. And she knew she'd hurt him. She knew the sound of her name in his voice the way she knew that curve in his back where she laid my head during the night, where she rested. She was on the verge of tears. "What about that make-up mirror? The one that's in your travel pack. I saw it."

He was chopping garlic and tomatoes now. He waited, didn't

look up, but finally said, "I use it to look at my bald spot. Eliot, I'm not as young as I used to be."

She considered this. Too easy. "Oh, and you think *that* explains it!"

He didn't look at her; he kept chopping. "Explains what?"

And he'd been going to the gym more often. Why, he'd even lost a few pounds! The out-of-love-in-love syndrome. She knew. "Hah!"

"Eliot, what are you thinking?"

"I'm certainly not thinking that you're *bald*."

"Have you *looked* at my bald spot lately?"

"No, but ..." She dabbed her eyes with a tissue from her pocket.

"But what? Eliot, answer me."

"But the make-up?" Why even ask this question? She could imagine. Was he standing on a sand dune when the screen door closed? Did the redhead disappear into the shadows of the darkened house, shades pulled against the sun to keep the cottage cool? Did he watch? Hope she'd go into the bedroom, raise the shade and light her mirror on the table where her make-up lay? Did he see her look at her face the way Eliot had once looked in a mirror?—the way Eliot had watched herself touch a finger to her lip and recalled how she'd once touched *his* lip, that quick light move, and how she'd slipped her slender finger inside his cool dry palm, the man who'd been her lover.

Max filled her hand with chopped garlic. "Eliot, this is embarrassing. It gets sunburned up there and I think it looks silly. A red spot in the middle of my head?"

Going, going, gone, Eliot thought. Like the moment of perfect timing, traveling so fast you might die, matter into energy—gone with the flash of light. She stood on her tiptoes, her free hand on his shoulder for leverage so she could see the back of his head. "Sunscreen?" she said.

"The garlic?" Max asked. "Eliot, pay attention," he ordered.

She tossed it into the hot oil in the pan. It sizzled faster than any garlic she'd ever cooked before. She had to be quick, get the tomatoes in there or the garlic would burn, find some basil. Had he bought any? "Basil?" she asked.

"In the bag, still. I'll wash it and chop it. You stir. You cook in your new kitchen, at your brand-new stove. You cook. Oh, Eliot, I love it when you cook."

This time she heard the sound of Max, the way he'd sigh after she'd made angel hair pasta with pesto, after she'd roasted the chicken with caramelized carrots and onions, after she'd placed in front of him her first fork-stirred omelet lightly dusted with white cheddar cheese before she'd rolled it onto his plate.

She shook her copper pan and heard the sound of her kitchen, tomatoes and basil sizzling on her hot fire, dinner about to be, and knew part of her was gone in all the kitchens she had known: gone—in the narrow house where she'd grown up, where her mother had skimmed from the boiling chicken the gray foam she'd tossed into the white porcelain sink; gone—in the kitchen she'd left for Max with its adobe tile floor she'd never thought she'd have and then thought she couldn't live without; gone—in the kitchen so small Max rigged up a pot rack for the shiny pots with a thin layer of copper inside the bottoms that made her a pro and that he'd bought for her when he moved in, but they were always in the way; gone—in the one kitchen she'd never seen, where her lover and his wife chopped tomatoes and cucumbers on a butcher block she imagined he'd built in the shop behind his farmhouse on the land where she was sure he'd grown the vegetables in a field of lavender because that was the scent of him in memory, ineffable and gone.

"Eliot, come here," Max said, and she did.

Losing

My father bought his first car in 1938. Six hundred and seven dollars cash on the barrel head got him a shiny black Ford and two lessons. He drove home, pulled up along the curb and watched his father-in-law, my grandfather Aaron Roseman, who'd been sitting on the marble stoop, cigar in hand, hobble down the path and step up on the running board.

Aaron Roseman never drove a car. He was barely five-feet tall and had a club foot. That and his life as a tailor, the trade he brought with him from Russia, the land he left because he was a Jew, made him hard-edged, tight with money and with words. He lit cigars in the fireplace with charred wood matches saved in a jar on the mantle. He had a telephone, proof of how far he'd come, and a safe in the wall, fire-proof evidence of what he'd come from.

My father used to sit on the hill in Patterson Park after school, across from Aaron Roseman's narrow brick house on Baltimore Street, and watch my mother's hips sway back and forth as she scrubbed the white marble steps. He knew the way she moved before he knew the feel of her. He knew the path she took from

Eastern High to home. He could tell her by her walk before her shape formed in his vision. And he began to walk beside her on the cobblestones that angled through old trees heavy with the heated light of summer, like his heart.

Aaron said, "Freda, he's poor, no profession, a schlepper."

"Gerson works hard, Papa."

"With feet," Aaron said, and turned away.

Gerson sold shoes, earned five dollars a week and gave one dollar to his mother. One whole week he ate donuts for lunch so he could buy two tickets to City High School's play. Freda held the tickets in her palm, turned them over with perfect, slender fingers so unlike his broad thick hand, and said she couldn't go. He went alone. In his hand inside his pocket he kept the extra ticket that she'd held.

And he took another path across the park.

Two years passed.

He was standing outside Felzer's shoe store on North Gay Street, taking a break. He crushed his cigarette under his foot, looked from the rubbed ash to Emory Zigler's size 11 polished black oxford. Emory, a pool hall buddy from his high school hanging-on-the-corner days, punched him in the arm, "Hey, Gersh, Al Lesser's got an opening. You know his store next to the Red Wing Movie Theater on Monument Street? He's puttin' shoes right out on the floor on a rack, just one shoe for each style. The girls can touch the shoes," said Emory, "but none of them can get their toes inside." Emory laughed. "He puts out the four and a halves." Freda's size, thought Gerson, remembering her tiny hands and feet, the way her head, if she should ever lean against him, would fit beneath his shoulder. "Lesser's sellin' them at $2.49 a pair. Go over there. Move up from this $1.95 schlock you're pushin'. The shoes are sellin' themselves." Emory turned to go, "And I guess you've heard about Freda Roseman?"

She'd been in the rumble seat of her brother-in-law's car

when it crashed. He went to see her in the hospital. He put his hand on her forehead, white and clear like the ivory silk of his tallit. And when he held her hand, he felt the shards of glass beneath her skin and thought about the hurt inside him while they'd been apart.

So once again they walked across the park. But now he took her small, bare hand and warmed it with his own.

The day of the wedding Aaron opened the door for Gerson, who wore the black suit my mother had bought him. The white summer suit she'd also bought was in the shopping bag he carried, along with everything else he owned. Aaron stepped aside to let him in but did not speak.

Three years later, when my grandmother was blind and Aaron's heart was ailing, he opened his door again for Gerson, suitcases in hand this time and Freda at his side. Aaron said, "I owe you, Gerson, for this mitzvah." Gerson bowed his head and wondered how they'd find the way to live together.

It was a silent partnership until the day my father bought the Ford. He needed the car for his new job selling insurance door-to-door. He figured the two lessons that came with the car were enough. He stalled at every traffic light but made it home and pulled up to the curb, breathing hard from the work of learning what the lessons had left out.

Aaron leaned on the rolled down window and said to Gerson, "Can you drive the thing?" Gerson thought about the gearshift H, wondered if he could get it into first again, and said, "Get in, let's see." He drove the old man from Baltimore Street to my Aunt Besse's house on Ulman Avenue, where my mother kneaded shabbat challahs in Besse's big wide kitchen. Then all hell broke lose. My mother and my aunt shouted at them both.

"How could you drive the old man?"

"Gerson, you could've killed Papa and yourself."

"Meshugah, meshugah."

"What were you thinking?"

Aaron said, "Let's take another turn around the block." In the rearview mirror, my father saw them in their aprons, a semaphore of arms white with baking flour, waving above their heads to stop the rolling wheels.

Aaron told Gerson to clean out the old carriage shed in the alley behind the house on Baltimore Street. "Put the Ford inside," he said. On Sundays Gerson carried Freda's bucket full of soapy water, set it on the ground, then backed the Ford out in the alley. Aaron supervised. "Careful now. A little to the left. Slower, slower. Ger-shon, Ger-shon. You'll scratch the fender. Cut the wheel tighter, harder. Ach, at last you've got it," he'd yell. But Gerson never got the hang of backing up. So Aaron was essential for the ritual of the washing.

One day, my father says, Aaron, who never carried a dish from the table to the sink, who never made himself a cup of tea, came outside with rag in-hand. Their hands bumped inside the soapy bucket. When they were done that day, they stood together in the alley and looked at their reflections in the sheen. My father, tall and thin. Aaron, small and bent with age. Aaron took a folded piece of paper from his pocket. "Here's the combination to my safe," he said. "You be the one to open it when I'm gone."

My father drove that car, and many others, all paid for with cash, in full, until he was eighty-three years old. He drove to collect premiums house by house, to sell policies for new couples, for new babies, for insurance against disaster. He drove my mother in early labor with my sister to Dr. Gutmacher's office. He put her in the car, but in his haste and anxiety smashed her finger in the door. Dr. Gutmacher tended to the finger, timed the contractions, and said, "Gerson, I'll drive her to the hospital. You follow." That was the only time he didn't drive one of us when things mattered. Whenever I saw a big dog outside, my father saved me with a ride to grade school. He drove me back to College Park after weekends at home my whole freshman year at the university when I was just sixteen, lonely and scared to live away. He drove my sister to the hospital when she lost her leg to diabetes. He drove my mother to the store for groceries and waited in the car while she picked out sweet-smelling melons. After her stroke, he dragged her wheelchair in and out of his big gray Chevy. And he drove to the cemetery every year between Rosh Hashanah and Yom Kippur to visit my mother's grave, and then later my sister's grave as well.

He never ran a red light. He got one speeding ticket when he and my mother were driving through a small town in Vermont on vacation. A policeman drove out from behind a billboard. "Didn't see that 15-mile speed limit sign, now did ya?" he said.

But last year my father missed a turn he always makes on his way to the Pikesville Senior Center. He made an illegal U-turn to get back to where he knew the way. The young policeman—and think how young this one looked to him that day—asked him to step outside the car and then laid down a wide strip of tape.

"Do you think I'm drunk?" my father asked.

"No sir, I don't. But I wonder why your hand shook so when you handed me your license."

"Getting stopped by the police can shake the nerves," my father said.

"Yes, sir, it can. Now, if you'll just step out."

My father's back is curved, his legs are stiff, his arms have thinned. He uses his hands to lift his legs above the floorboard of the car when he gets out.

He walked the policeman's line with a shuffle in his gait. The years dragged on his foot.

While the policeman wrote the ticket that took away his license, my father stood in summer heavy sun and watched his shadow shimmer on the tar. He thought of his tallit and how he used to sit in synagogue and watch the fringes swing in sunlight, and the threads of memory flickered in his head.

He thought of the day so long ago when Aaron stepped up on the running board, and then of the day they put the old man in the ground—the day he opened up the safe. Aaron, crippled all his life, who left, instead of cash, a pile of IOUs signed by relatives and friends who'd seen bad times, old pieces of paper from worn out lives saved like burnt matchsticks in a jar. Aaron, who made sure my father was the one to stand before the open safe, to hold the papers in his hands. Aaron, who knew that he would throw them all away.

Madness and Folly

O livia heard the story of the harpist on the radio, while she was in her car driving to the hospital the day after the operation, after her father's hip had been repaired, after the plate and screw had been placed inside and his skin had been stapled together—a long line of staples from the muscular curve of his hip down to the middle of his thigh. She saw the wound like the string of a harp and the staples like the forked disks that lie against the string, that twist against the string when the pedal is moved from flat to natural, that tighten the string. She saw his whole body as a harp and the seam that was healing as one long string with the sound of one note that she would hear in a long orchestral piece. This made no sense to her, but it was how she saw it.

Now, in this same incongruous way, she was thinking about jokes.

Jokes everywhere, she thought when she parked the car, entered the hospital, smelled the alcohol in the linoleum halls, took the elevator to her father's private room where he would tell her jokes.

Yesterday he'd told an understated joke when the surgeon asked him in the pre-op conference outside the operating room,

"What are you allergic to, Mr. Berenson?"

"Orchard grass," her father said with a straight face.

Dr. Schwartz, the surgeon, looked blankly at her eighty-five-year-old father and Olivia read the disinterest in his eyes.

"Get the orchard grass out of the operating room!" Martha, the surgical nurse, said. And Olivia and her father laughed while Dr. Schwartz curved his lips in a tolerant smile. Olivia would never see this nurse again, but she would remember how tall she was, as tall as the doctor, six feet. She would remember her stature, the way she remembered the harpist who came into her head when her father—out of his head—told jokes.

He had not told jokes the week before he fell. He took her hand, and said, "There's an inevitability about the present."

She understood the way she'd understood when her mother, four years after her stroke, decided not to eat when the new year came, when she took Olivia's hand and said "Yitgadal v'yitkadash"—the first two words of the mourner's kaddish. Five years later, her father took her hand on a hot day in June.

They'd been sitting in the house with the old round Toastmaster fan blowing at their feet, humming the way old memories did inside her head. They'd been talking about the kind of housing called assisted living. "Assisted living," he said. "Funny term. Either you're living or you're not, right?"

She didn't answer.

"I'm on my way down," her father said. "I know that. This is just a stopover."

"Stopover from what to what?"

"Don't get philosophical on me, kid."

Her father's eyes were brown like hers. She saw them full of light from the sun that angled through the window. She saw the green and yellow—the colors of her mother's hazel eyes—there inside the brown.

She remembered the dream she had after her mother died. In

a haze of yellow light, her mother in a flowered housedress. Olivia couldn't tell the color of her hair—pure white when she died. But it must be dark—around her face in finger-placed waves, how it was when Olivia could still fit beneath her arm, lean against her curve of breast. Then an empty chair. An elegant, suited man on the sidewalk. Her mother, on the stoop of their row house. Her arm raised high in dance position. No one stands inside her hold. She leans to unheard sound. She turns round. A fox-trot circle. Olivia's father threads eight-millimeter film through the projector, on the wheel. A home movie. Overexposed. Her mother. Like the whiteness of a leafing tree against night sky.

"Why are you crying?" her father said. "This won't be the last time you see me."

"It's what I do. I cry, easily, often."

"So do I," he said. "It's inherited."

The day after the surgery, Olivia arrived on the heels of today's joke: he was arguing with Joanne, the floor nurse, "I have to get up, leave. Now."

"Mr. Berenson, you've had an operation. You can't move your leg. You broke your hip."

"Go off on something else," he said.

Joanne and Olivia looked at one another. Joanne said, "Things are about the same as yesterday."

"Back to it," he said.

"Back to what, Daddy?"

"Get my clothes."

Back and forth they went like Abbott and Costello asking one another, "Who's on first?" Joanne repeated. He repeated. A litany of dialogue. Olivia recited, "You broke your hip. It has to heal."

Joanne threw up her hands. "Okay, Mr. Berenson, I give up. Get up, leave."

He fixed Joanne with a dead stare. "I can't leave. I've broken my hip." The expression on his face: What, are you nuts?

A joke. A jokester. Feste, the jester.

The harpist said to the interviewer on NPR, "I ran away from home when I was sixteen." "With your harp?" the interviewer said. "Why, yes, of course," said the harpist with a light brogue. Beside her father's bed, Olivia imagined her. The harp strapped to her back. Or struggling to fit it up the narrow stairs of a bus, angling it onto a train, propping it through the sunroof of a car. Or dragging it on a dolly—rigged up on childhood roller skates and a wooden platform, pulling the harp behind her with a rope. Like a joke.

Olivia hadn't understood, at first, that her father was telling jokes. He'd come down from the recovery room sitting upright on the gurney. Wild-eyed as if he saw no one. "Get me out of here," he'd screamed, his blank eyes on Olivia. He took her hand. "Get me out of here." His grip tight, hard on the narrow bones of her palm, her fingers.

"Daddy." His grip tightened. He'd never hurt her.

"Do something," he said.

The green-eyed nurse—Olivia didn't yet know her name the day of the surgery—and the black orderly with the colored African cap had used the sheets from the gurney to move her father onto the bed.

"I want out of here," he'd shouted while they dragged him on the sheets.

"Is he getting something for pain?" Olivia shouted.

"I want my clothes, my pants, my shirt, my shoes, I want to go home, I want out of here."

Olivia found the nurse's name on her ID card, clipped to the pink edge of her hospital shirt. "Joanne," she said. Joanne McGregor, she read. But Joanne didn't answer. She was setting up her father's IV to the automatic pump. She was poking in numbers or words, making the machine beep. She was turning the small plastic device on the tube, adjusting the drip.

"Call the police," he yelled.

"Do you know me?" Olivia asked.

"Don't fool with me. Olivia, Olivia," he shouted. "I know you. Do you know *me*? Call the police. Dial 911."

"Joanne." This name—Olivia made louder and louder—all she could think to do. She didn't think she could tell jokes.

She went home and lay down in bed with her husband. She didn't call their only child, Deborah, in Manhattan, who might have come to Baltimore to help. She couldn't talk. She ate the food Mishel brought to her in bed: the Russian chicken burgers, the beets, the rice, the stroganoff sauce she'd made before her father had fallen in his house and broken his hip—or had his hip broken and then he'd fallen? "It can happen that way," Dr. Schwartz had said in the emergency room. Things backwards, reversed. Like a joke, she thought as she lay down, as Mishel curled himself around her.

She slept, dreaming she wins a prize for an article she's written for a newspaper in Annapolis because it contains a reference to Duncan. (Duncan appears in the dream to be a place near Annapolis or a famous Maryland person, either one, the way dreams work.) She is reading the piece out loud, but everyone in the audience is deaf.

When Olivia was awake, she worked as a reporter for the *Baltimore Sun*. Before her father broke his hip, she was working on an article about the deaf, interviewing students and teachers at

Galludet College. She'd been thinking about the fact that sign language exists when two people stand in front of one another using it. Present. Simple verbs signed: Go. Come. The past and future on an imaginary timeline.

Olivia awoke trying to remember who Duncan could be. The only Duncan she'd heard of was the king Macbeth killed. She was alarmed at murder hidden in a layer beneath her dream. She decided, I can't finish the piece on the deaf. My present is gone.

Was Nabokov wrong when he said, *One is always at home in one's past?*

She began seeing the red-haired Irish girl—her face, her green eyes, her long, slim, strong body, her long hair, its curls and waves tangled with her harp strings. She began seeing the harpist, whose voice she'd heard on the radio, whenever she was with her father.

Now her father pulled off his gown, exposing himself. "I have my schmuck out here and you women are in the room." He threw the gown on the floor. Olivia could see the wound, the bruising—purple, blue, red, yellow—down the seam, down his leg, into his swollen ankle. She could see the catheter like an amber straw coming out of the center of his penis. She'd never seen his penis before. He pulled on the catheter.

"No," Joanne shouted. "Mr. Berenson, we'll hurt you if we have to put it in again. Mr. Berenson, you can't walk to the bathroom."

"Daddy, please." Olivia took his hand.

He put her hand in his mouth. "I'll bite it. I'll bite it off. I'll make you bleed."

"Go ahead," she shouted, the warmth of his mouth, the little buds of his tongue on her hand, his teeth on her skin. With his lips closed on her hand, he raised his eyes to hers. Wild, angry.

She waited for the bite but he opened his mouth, let her hand drop.

She saw the hand of the harpist reach toward the beautiful wood frame of the harp, saw her hand reach toward the curve of the polished wood neck, saw her adjust the tuning peg, press the shoulder of the harp to her own, and reach for one single string.

"Women handling my penis. Are you whores?" He looked at Joanne. "Take your clothes off."

"What?"

"Take *off* your clothes."

"Mr. Berenson, I'd like to know why you want me to do that."

The two women waited. A comedic pause.

"To see what you look like without them."

Olivia said to her father, "Did you know that the nylon string of the harp is almost six feet, the height of a man?" The height of her father, the doctor, the nurse in the operating room. She said, "Four thousand, four hundred pounds." She was referring to the pressure of the strings, of one finger that plucks one string, one note, on the sounding board, when the harp is tuned to the correct pitch. She saw no need to explain it to her father—the jokester.

"Right," he said. "The pressure is rising." He pointed to the IV pump, to the headline that ran across its top like a tiny replica of the gigantic marquee in Times Square. She read the words: the pressure limit is 400 millimeters. "The pressure limit has been exceeded," he said, "about to explode."

At home, she threw her purse into the foyer, turned it upside down, emptied it in a fury of keys and lipstick, pouches with makeup, pencils, address book, candy wrapped in cellophane, Tampax, bits of Kleenex fluff, dust, and pennies on the foyer floor.

Mishel came out of the kitchen, still in his suit, the mail in his hands. "What are you doing? What's wrong with you? Talk to me."

"No," she screamed. "No, no."

"You're tired," he said. "Come."

"Like pennies tossed away, rolling on the floor, spitting from my purse."

"What?" he asked.

"I don't know," she said. "Wheelchairs."

She went into the bathroom, pulled at the wiry strands of gray that streaked her head and in the mirror, told herself, "I'm a hoary-headed, old woman like my mother at the end. I'm in danger. But of what?" and then she went to bed.

When she woke, she didn't want to go to the hospital. She wanted to go to New York to see Deborah. She wanted to go shopping. She wanted to go to work. But after breakfast, after Mishel had gone to work—he'd let her sleep, and it was late—she called her boss and told him she wouldn't be in again today. "I don't know when," she told him.

At the hospital, she told her father jokes.

When she arrived, he said, "Which way is out?"

"Henny Youngman would know."

"Right, take my wife."

"Somebody already did."

He was silent. Olivia waited. Did he remember?

"Take my wife—please."

Well, he remembered that. So she said, " Remember this one? Woman goes into a bar with a pig under her arm. Bartender says, 'Where'd you get that ugly thing?' Pig says, 'I won her in a raffle.'"

"You're ugly," he said.

"Yes."

In the hospital parking lot she told herself this joke: "She was born on April second. A day late."

In the morning she brought the "box," the CD player from his house, in the hope that music would reach him—or her. She stood and watched him. He was curled on his side, the blanket askew over the wound that lay like a harp string on his thigh— how she saw it, tight, pulled, stapled. Nailed. With his right hand, he rhythmically banged on his heart. But she heard no music and played none.

She'd seen him do this in shul to the recitation of sins on Yom Kippur—the *Al Khet*. Each line begins with these words, *for sins*, followed by acts of wrongdoing, and with these words her father would hit his chest.

But this is not what Olivia recalled as she watched him sleeping, though that image lay hidden and visible like the wound that lay before her, covered and uncovered.

She was six, her father was in the rocker in her parents' bedroom, his hand on his heart, weeping. He was so big. Only children cry, she'd thought and grasped her own small chest. His brother, her uncle, had died.

Now she slipped a CD in the player and watched her father wake to the slow piano of the "Pathétique's" adagio, watched him turn onto his back, watched the wound disappear beneath the sheet, watched his hand lie still on his heart, his eyes open—and the tears. She took a tissue, wiped his eyes.

He grabbed her wrist, held it tight.

She said, "Did you know that the harpist in the orchestra mimed, pretended, the ping of her one note in the long orchestral piece, and her teacher, the conductor, said, 'Lovely, dear'?"

He pulled her head down onto his chest and in her ear, he whispered, "The plot thickens."

She gave in to him, bent her back and laid her head on his chest, that big wide chest where she'd sought comfort as a child and as a woman. He kept her wrist in his hand and, with her other hand, she hit her chest and said, "Al khet."

"For sins committed," he said.

"And that she knew, then, that she must go?" she said into his chest.

"Under duress," he said.

She stood, and he let go of her wrist.

"There's no music," he said.

The "Pathetique" was in the last movement, the allegro.

"No," she agreed, "no music."

"No ping," he said.

Olivia could see the harpist running away, the harp on her back. She left her father's hospital room.

In the parking lot, she sat in her car.

Feste the jester said, "The lady bade take away the fool, therefore, I say again, take her away."

The lady said, "Sir, I bade them take away you."

The jester said, "Give me leave to prove you a fool."

The harpist said, "Come."

To Swim?

The rabbis have said a father must circumcise his son to redeem him and, some also say, to teach him to swim. To swim? My father had no sons.

I think about this question: if you come to a small body of water, would you take a boat, walk around, or swim across? I was in a small motor boat the day my father died. He was not near the water, he was not in the boat, he could not walk.

To swim? The rabbi's student asks.

I think about this question: if a married woman, whose father had died, dreamed of another man and that man said, "Swim to me," should she?

To swim?

His life may depend on it, the rabbi says.

In the morning when Ben touched her, placed his hand ever so gently on her white cotton turtleneck that she wore nothing under, that she'd pulled over her head for a quick cup of coffee before her shower, when he placed his hand on her breast, she became so quickly aroused that she was frightened, for she thought she didn't love Ben the way she used to, that maybe she'd never had the kind of erotic feeling for him that she had for the man in her head. And then Ben had failed, the usual male failure, because, he said, he'd wanted her too much.

Lying next to him, she conjured up the dream man. The man was a beautiful dark-haired man. She could see his face now. His eyes were small, brown, with almost the angle and narrowness of an Asian eye, though it was not.

Her father had loved the beauty of Asian women, their smallness, lightness of bone, like her own bones and body structure though she was very fair, did not have the mellow beige Asian color in her skin, but still her hair was deep and dark, almost black with a hint of auburn when light shone on it, or so her father had said.

The man was quite tall, more than six feet, not perfectly built, his hips too small for his frame, his thighs too large. He was no longer fit and flat in the abdomen the way young men are. But then she too was no longer young. She loved the color in his skin. Once she'd seen an old tree during a summer drought with a few leaves that seemed to have forgotten the season and turned the color of fall in one or two odd places. Fiery red. That's what she saw in his skin, a blush on his chest, the color of sex. At times, he had a moist glow like the sheen of sun and a frisson of oil on water—the light she'd seen on the lake the day of the picnic, the day her father had died. Nothing about him repelled her. Everything about him seemed erotic: the fullness of his lips, the length of his fingers, the narrowness of his feet, which seemed delicate and beautiful to her. Strong delicate feet. Rich dark hair on his head, tiny curled body hairs.

She had not touched him. And if she could? What would happen?

He seemed both alive and dormant, old and new. He reminded her of a tree. Rooted in her consciousness.

At breakfast Ben told her his dream. He said he'd been in a room with action-hero movie stars: Clint Eastwood, Charles Bronson, Robert DeNiro. He said he'd been wearing a strange hat with a long narrow brim that extended forward and that when he'd walked into the room, the brim had grazed the cheek of Clint Eastwood and that Eastwood had then talked to him.

"Any good dialogue?" she asked.

"Well, I told Clint I heard he was making a new movie about a boy in a war—I don't know which war—and an older man, maybe the boy's father. I told him it sounded good."

"Did Clint have anything to say?" She wanted to ask about the father? What did Clint say about him? But this was Ben's dream, not hers.

"No, or I can't remember."

"So, no good dialogue."

"Right," Ben said. "But why was I in this room with these movie stars?"

"You were dreaming." Not the way she dreamed. Nightmares about her father, daydreams about the other man. She could see the dream man—now, right now while she talked with Ben. She envied her husband—he dreamed at night like a normal person. She was no longer completely sure when she was dreaming and when she was not. But she needed to know. She took herself too seriously; she knew that. So she said, "But what is the meaning of the hat?"—in her mind, with that question, she made the dream both serious and silly, perhaps a way to help him (or her?) with this morning's failure, so to speak.

"Yes," Ben said and he laughed, "the hat. What is the mean-ing of the hat?"

Dream man. I'll give my dream man a hat, she thought.

Why was this man in her head when still she desired Ben, wanted to make love to him? Maybe Ben's dream could help them both. She said, "Let's make up a story about the hat. Will you play?"

"Oh, why not," he said, "You're so good at this stuff. Maybe you can figure out my dream."

But now the hat—her joke about his dream, her way of easing them into the game—was in the dream man's hand. A long brim, a baseball cap like Ben's, the one he'd bought at the Matanzas Creek winery when they were in Sonoma, the one he wore to the picnic. Above the brim, the name Santa Rosa, the town where the vineyards lay, was spelled out in red. She liked the way the red reminded her of the flush on his chest. The dream man put on Ben's black baseball cap. Ben wouldn't miss the hat. He had so many, and she often wore this one in the rain because it was black like her slicker. She thought of it as her own.

"Why don't we try to figure it out?" Ben said.

She wanted to figure out why she had a made-up lover during the day. She wanted to feel sane, reliable, good. Her moral framework had been disturbed by the dreams that occurred while she was awake, because she couldn't stop them. She *deserved* the nightmares.

Last night when she'd slid into bed next to Ben, she'd received a call from the other man—a dream man call. He said, "Your phone won't answer?"

"What do you mean?" she asked. She knew his voice, soft and throaty.

He said, "I let it ring five times. That's what I mean."

"It needs to ring seven times for the service to pick up." She had no service. What was she talking about?

After my father died, I saw him in a dream. He was wearing shorts and tennis shoes, and he told me he loved my black dress with the spaghetti straps. He touched my hair and then got into a row boat. I knew he was dead and asked him, "Will you come again?" He didn't answer.

When I woke, all I could think of was the woman in the Bible whose seven sons were slain. How she didn't know how to mourn, for whom to rend her hair. And then I thought of me in the motor boat.

How could I have been in that boat?

"I need you," the dream man said.

She loved when he flattered her, but often chose not to respond. She liked being in control. She needed him more than he knew, but she was tired, needed to sleep. "I'm beat."

He said—he often spoke to her in non sequiturs—"If you come to a small body of water, would you walk around, swim across, or take a boat?"

She said, "Swim. But my father is taking the boat."

My father was old when he died, sick and old. It was time and I knew it.

From his wheelchair my father reached his crooked arm— bent with age and immobility and Parkinson's disease—around my head that I'd laid on his thin thigh, above the knee that was also frozen in the same bent angle of his arm. He said, "I'll mess your hairdo," because his fingers that he could no longer move dug into my scalp—an embrace that felt like bones, like the pull of the grave.

I visited him every day. He held me this way every time. He always said something about my hair. "That's a good haircut." Or just, "Your hair."

"Okay, I'll start," said Ben. He sat, elbow on the table, chin in his hand.

She knew he couldn't think of anything, and she couldn't tell him what she'd been thinking.

"But I'm no good at this," he said. "You start."

She tried to make up something but recalled instead a morningmare, the nightmares that she'd re-termed because they came in the morning. These terrors woke her the way nightmares wake their victims, but were more memorable because they occurred right before she started her day—so vivid, she couldn't get them out of her mind. In each one, something terrible and erotic happened to her. She was punished when she slept. Perhaps for the daydreams?

In this morning's, her father appears with some strange awful thing in his mouth, many colored. Is he dead or alive? She doesn't know. The thing is large, long, wrinkled, with rings of fleshlike skin—or is it plastic? The color is orange-brown and then reds, yellows, circle round and round. As she comes closer, she becomes more frightened. She thinks he has an oversized, deformed penis in his mouth. Is he dead or alive? She doesn't know. She knows that he is circumcised, though she cannot see the end of his penis.

She hadn't told Ben about the morningmares. Certainly she couldn't tell him about the dream man.

"Clint had had a nightmare about his new movie," she said. "All his actors were wearing hats. All kinds of hats, and they wouldn't take them off. When he tried to pull one off, it turned out to be a part of the person's head."

"They were deformed?"

"Their hats revealed stuff. They couldn't hide anything the way normal people can." She was worried that she was like them, that she couldn't hide her dream man. He was coming when she was awake, conscious, and she couldn't stop him. Why, he might be visible to others. To Ben? Her terrors made sense to her. Everybody gets them now and then. Maybe Ben's dream had been a nightmare. People remember their nightmares. They're the dreams we talk about. That's why Ben told her. No, she couldn't tell him hers.

The other day she'd been in an elevator when a woman said to a man, "I dreamed about my old boyfriend. You know, the one I finally got to stop calling. And there he was in my dream. I couldn't get rid of him. It was awful."

"And Clint was wearing a hat, too," said Ben, "a baseball cap. But Clint's hat was magic, right?"

"Of course, it had to be a magic hat," she said. "Are there any others?"

Ben laughed. "No one wears hats since Kennedy refused to wear one at the inauguration. Only baseball caps. They're everywhere. You know how I love my baseball caps." He had a collection of them, wore them to ballgames, when he mowed the lawn, when he took his kayak out.

He'd taken his kayak out that day they went to the eastern shore for the picnic. He'd paddled across from the pier to the island where the hot dogs and barbecued chicken smoked on the charcoal grills, to where the blueberry and apple pies sat ready on white paper cloths, to all the food her father could no longer hold in his crooked hands, could no longer cut with a knife and fork, could no longer grab and bite, or drop into his open mouth with his head back—a voracious, joyful toss of that last bite of hot dog and bun—the way she'd seen him do all her life. She rode with others from Ben's office in the motor boat and had watched Ben, out there alone. She'd wished she could have joined him, but it was a one-man boat and she knew nothing about kayaks.

That's what I need, she thought now, *a one-man boat, a way to get away, surrounded by water.* She wasn't alone when she slept. She wasn't alone when she was awake. She thought if she could be alone, she could be safe. Or if she could be with the dream man.

The dream man said to her, "Will you swim across, take the boat, or walk around?"

"To get to you, you mean?"

He said, "Your father is in the boat."

"And he died," she said.

My father didn't die in a boat.

On the day of the picnic, I told him I had to go home to cook dinner. I lied and then I got into a boat. Before I left, he said, "I want you to go. I know it's good for you, but I'm afraid you'll abandon me." Why did he say this?

He knew, didn't he?

The dream man said, "Then swim to me. Meet me." It didn't seem necessary to say where. He took her to a room that was large, painted white. Light came into the room in some way she couldn't discern. There was no window. This light gave the room an amber cast. A defined, windowless space that no one could look into. She felt safe even though she couldn't really tell where the room began and ended. After they entered, he said, "It's safe here and the day is long, a day for you." He'd told her she should dress for him. She had not asked how. She knew. She wore elegant clothes: beige panties, the Asian beige she imagined her father loved, matching beige bra, smooth across the nipple, no seams. She wore a summer-weight, white cashmere sweater, the material luxuriously soft to the touch and so thin that her bra, her narrow shoulders, could be seen. Yet when the sweater, a startling white—the white, a striking contrast to the black and the smooth muted sheen of the silk trousers she wore, the ones that flared ever so slightly at the ankle—when the sweater extended over the waistband—actually these trousers had no waistband, but met smoothly in a hook and eye and zipper in the center of her back, like the line between her buttocks—the sweater rolled slightly, the roll of an unfinished edge, at the bottom because the weave was so delicate. The dream man wore a pair of black slacks, a dark taupe shirt with a dark tie. The button at the neck was open in this way he had of wearing his tie knotted close to the neck, but with that button still open. This way he had of doing this made her want to touch his neck, to skim her finger across the little hairs there.

The bed in the room was large and white. It was covered with a summer-weight comforter. He carefully turned the bed down and asked her to feel the mattress. It had a thick, deep quilted mattress cover under the fine cotton sheet.

The dream man took off his hat and made love to her by removing each piece of her clothing so slowly that she would try to help him get the sweater off or the trousers, but he said, "No," and continued to move his hands and to kiss her body in lip-wide measures of revealed skin until he had kissed every part as he removed the article of clothing. Then he would stop and admire: he told her how the sweater material felt to him—"smooth and light." He said, even though he had not yet placed his hands on her skin, "I know how you feel beneath it. I know your skin and the feel of your heartbeat." When she was naked, he removed his shirt and said, "Let's lie now with our hearts together. Let's see if we can hear each other's beat." And they did, nipple to nipple. He wrapped one arm around her narrow chest and reached his hand to her breast. He said, "Only you can I hold this way."

My father must have wrapped his arm around my back this way when I was a small child, in the way that a large man would carry a little girl who was tired and needed badly to sleep, so tired; I can recall how my chest would press against his and how safe the pounding beneath his great chest, so large against my own, made me feel.

I think my father knew I wanted to abandon him. Did he know that I asked myself what he had to offer me now, to give me? That I felt he wanted too much from me? My mother's and my sister's slow, painful, anguished deaths filled my years with long linoleum hospital halls, while my father sat in the orange chairs in the waiting places for the families of the sick. While he sat distant, apart, I went to the gurneys and the bedsides. I walked down the halls to the elevators that led to the operating room where one day they cut off my sister's leg. While I held my mother's hand and felt the blood inside her fingers slow as if the blood that bled into her brain came from that hand, reversed and went another way, took a wrong turn, and that left her hand crooked and bent like his, while I went with her to the room where they put her in a tube to look inside her brain, to confirm the stroke, the bleeding in her brain, while I did that, while she lay in the tube unconscious, he sat in an orange chair in a waiting room.

I think now, Why were those chairs, plastic-leather-cushioned or hard-curved-molded in all the rooms where he waited, all orange? Like the unexplained orange on the forehead in the Kunitz poem: "the night nailed like an orange to my brow." My father was nailed to my brow. He sat in his wheelchair with his arm around my head. Bent and angled bones that would not straighten out. I felt no blood coursing through him, no soft flesh pressing down on mine.

No way out.

The way he felt while he sat in the orange chairs?

The dream man removed his trousers and his boxers. He was circumcised (this was important to her). She needed to stop, to talk
with him. She said, "I know that if we make love, if you're really
here, you'll lose interest." Or would I? she asked herself.

And he answered with decided certainty that alarmed, confused her. "I suppose it's possible that this would happen. In the
realm that anything is possible. But do you see evidence that it
might happen? I suppose it can be said that we haven't really
'acted out' the physical side, yet. But assuming we've been in the
neighborhood—" How had they been in the neighborhood? Did
thinking about it make it real? Had she committed adultery? The
anxiety rose in her chest as he spoke. "I don't feel any signs of
looking to another fantasy," he said.

Ah, she was his fantasy. She wasn't real. If she wasn't, he
wasn't. She could get rid of him.

She said, "Maybe I'm a gigantic larger-than-life dream for
you?" An arrogant thing to say. But he was this for her. And she
needed to separate herself from him. Give him her thoughts so
that he would go away. Projection, a word her husband used
often when they argued. "You say I don't desire you." Yes, she had
said that to Ben. No wonder he'd failed this morning. "You must
know," he'd say, "it's you who doesn't want me." "Projecting," he'd
say. It sounded official. A pronouncement. Like the doctor when
he said, "Parkinson's." Her father. "His joints, stiff, old," the doctor had said. Expert, knowing, final.

The dream man said, "While I would have argued that you
weren't larger than life, it appears that you may be."

But if he saw her aging thin body, he wouldn't want her.

Ben said, "Where are you? Are you still in the game?"

How long had she been away? He must see that she was day-
dreaming. Could he see the dream? "Where were we?" she said.

"Have you gone away?" she said to the dream man. But he didn't answer.

"The magic hat," Ben said. "His baseball cap."

She must try, make up something. Be here with Ben. She said, "Well, Clint's actors had these hats attached to their heads, but Clint had that magic baseball cap."

"I think," Ben said, "that Clint could make the deformities, you know, those hats that revealed stuff, go away. Don't you think?"

"But why wouldn't he want to know their thoughts?" she said. She wanted to ask, Do you know mine? Would it help me if you did? "Don't you think," she said, "he'd like to look inside and see what they were thinking?"

"Why would anyone really want to do that? I don't want to do that—even if I have the magic hat."

"Why not?"

"You, for example," he said.

"What?" she said. What did he know about her? Did he see the dream man?

"I don't want to know."

"You don't want to know what?"

"What? Nothing. Everything, sure, in a way," he said. "But not really. I don't know."

"Maybe not what, but what about who?" If he asked me now, maybe she could tell.

"Who? What are you talking about?"

But she couldn't tell. He'd never understand. Who could understand? "Who? What?" she said. Now she needed to deflect his question. "We sound like Abbott and Costello." And they did. She laughed and said, "Who's on first?"

He laughed. "Yeah, well who is?"

"Who, I think. What's on second. Oh, I can't remember." She wanted to say, but seriously. She wanted to go back to the dream. But whose? His or hers? She said instead, "Don't you want to know my story?"

"Stories end," Ben said.

The dream man sounded official. He said, "When one or the other says something that seems to place his arrangement/nonarrangement in question of further jeopardy, the other, in this instance, me, reacts. Even if that reaction is involuntary and irrational and of all things unnecessary. I know what I know—Paul Simon, 'Graceland'— and I know what you know, and what we know. We're at risk, at best, on the one hand. No, on both hands. I'm not falling apart here, though it may sound it."

It didn't sound it. But what was he talking about?

"It's just another reality check," he said. But he wasn't real. And he said "reality check" as if she needed one, the way Ben said "projecting" to make her see her mistakes. A tick, this phrase he used and the one Ben used, a tick unique to each but that had the same effect on her: caused her to halt, think, reassess. If only she could. He sounded expert when he said it. Like the doctor. "And I suppose," he continued, "reality runs up against fantasy."

"I'll end," she said to Ben.

"This is getting too serious. Come watch the game with me." The Orioles were playing the Mets. They were inveterate O's fans. "We'll drink wine and eat spicy Doritos. Be totally decadent. And you can talk all you want during the game." He never let her talk during a game—that was serious stuff to him— and he made her laugh, made her think he was seducing her. But once they were in bed with their wine, he didn't touch her and she was afraid to touch him, afraid he wouldn't want her. She'd never believed that he'd failed because he wanted her too much. She believed he failed because he no longer desired her. And why should he? She desired the man in her head—the dream man.

But Ben did say, "Now if I had that magic hat," and he clinked his glass to hers.

She did want him, and she put her hand on her own sex, inside her leggings. She felt erotic and wanted him to know. This is all she knew to do. He grabbed her hand, pulled it out, said, "Don't."

When my father died, the dream man called and went away; I couldn't see him. I didn't understand how he could come and then leave when I needed him. Here's how he did it. I sat shiva for seven days. And during this time, he called once—a dream man call—but I told him I couldn't be reached. But once during that week, he called again when I was alone—everyone in my family, after all, had died. It was not shiva the way I had remembered other shivas—my mother's, my sister's. My aunts and uncles. These last, like my mother's and sister's, the house full of people, but easier to get through because I hadn't loved them in that life-eating way that I loved my mother and my sister. That's how I felt when *they* died, while the visitors—so many more than came to my father's shiva—ate at the dining room table, as if they were eating me, as if the deaths had eaten my life, or was it the illnesses—my mother's stroke, my sister's diabetes—that had eaten me? I should answer that question. But I prefer to think about the way I'd told him during shiva that he *could* come.

"How could I do that?" he'd asked.

"Why, strangers come all the time," I told him. "But that's not the point. The point is that no one comes to this shiva the way people came to the other shivas. I sit alone. I sit and wait and do honor alone. But a man coming to my door wouldn't be seen as odd during this week." He'd called, I heard his voice, I figured I could see him if I asked. "Anyone can come to the door. The door is always unlocked during the day. I sit here alone with the door unlocked hoping that the mailman will walk in, that you will walk in, that I will be robbed, even. But no one comes. You could come."

"No," he said. Simply no—how could he simply say that and not explain?

Because Ben had pulled her hand away, she left the bed, pulled out the ironing board in the extra bedroom where their daughter, who was grown now, once slept. She ironed her mother's linen napkins and tablecloths, old worn linen that she had washed and whitened and now starched and ironed.

When she finished, she lay down on her daughter's bed and fell asleep—a nap midday, and a nightmare in the afternoon:

She is naked with Ben. She asks him to lie with his buttocks on her chest, his legs parted round her head. He does and she looks into his v and sees her own. She sees her labia, her clitoris, the opening to her vagina. This is the first time she has seen this part of her body...

Naked men always look at their sex. Circumcised men can see that they are circumcised and some know the reason for it: to redeem him and, also some say, to teach him to swim.

To swim?

After my father died, after the shiva was over, after I'd gone outside, walked around the block, I dreamed that my father came to a family dinner. "But you've just died," I said to him. He didn't answer. I'd seen him lying on a metal table in the funeral home.

I'd seen his head mounted, it seemed to me, but it was resting on a porcelain pedestal. How could he be at the dinner? But there he was, and he was fit and strong. He was slim and walking, not wheelchair-bound. He approached me after dinner and brought his face close to mine. He didn't have the sour breath of the aging, that acrid odor I'd taken in whenever I kissed him good-bye at the home where he was dying, where his skin had the moist cool look of, not sweat, but overuse. Now his breath was sweet with the dessert we'd eaten, his skin reminded me of the way he used to smell and look when I was a child and he'd just shaved. He never used a straight razor. He used an electric one and powdered his face with a round orange puff—I've always wondered if it had been my mother's—I have never seen powder like this again, don't know what it really is, wonder if memory made this up. But that is how he looked in the dream, smooth and lightly powdered with a masculine-perfumed air about him. The odor, seductive for me in that whenever I smell anything that seems like it—my husband's skin has always smelled like this unnameable odor—I become aroused. I wonder if it was his smell, a part of his young body the way it is a part of my husband's, that I remember or if it really was the powder. The powder, a cover for my desire for my father.

When Ben came into the bedroom—she was sleeping lightly—she woke and went back to the iron and the board. He was wearing his baseball cap—the black one. She said, "How could you have said that to me?" How could he have pulled at her hand? What should she do now? Then she said, before he could answer, "No, I deserved it."

"No," he said.

Simply that, No. Why didn't he explain? Didn't he understand what she deserved?

He said, "Whose hat is this anyway? You wear it all the time."

"I don't know."

"It's magic," he said.

"No, there's no magic."

"Maybe not. But who really knows?"

"I know."

"I know what I know," he said, "and I know it's magic."

He came toward her and she turned from him, bumped into the ironing board. The board fell, the iron fell, her mother's linens everywhere.

"The iron," she said.

"It's off. It goes off when it falls. A safety feature. Don't worry about it." He said, "You know who's on first? We're on first." And he put his hands on her head. "Your hair," he said and kissed her. Then he put the baseball cap on her head. He held her against his chest. He said, "I can feel your heart beat."

"My father," she said.

"What? What about him?"

"I want him. I need him."

"I know," he said and wrapped one arm around her back, reached all the way around, while he pressed his other hand to the back of her head.

And they made love on the floor in the room where their daughter, who was grown and gone away, had lain as a child. They made love, her mother's linens all around them, beneath them. She would have to wash and iron them again.

But then, right then, she had his skin next to hers and the scent of powder seduced her, though he never used powder.

I remember the boat I was in while my father died alone, without me. I remember how I had left him, how I knew that he was dying and how I left anyway, how I came back too late when he was gone, how I stood by his body, his face vulnerable in death, how I touched his hand, kissed his forehead—cool and smooth—how I said, "The rabbis say, 'The day is long and the task is hard.'" How I said, "Remember the woman in the Bible with seven sons, all slain, how she cried out, 'I don't know for whom I am to cry or for whom I am to disarray my hair?'" How I said, "I know." How I pulled at my hair that my father had loved.

I say out loud now: "If you come to a small body of water, would you walk around, swim across, or take a boat?" And I answer, "Swim."

Riptide

My mother died on a Wednesday. I sat in my room for a month after she died. I didn't go to my office. I didn't do my laundry. I didn't answer the phone. In Washington you can get most everything you need delivered by strangers, wearing caps, speaking with accents. I tried not to order twice from the same place. I didn't want to know anyone. I developed a kind of system. A delivery rotation system to make sure the one who came to the door wouldn't know me, even if I remembered him.

My answering machine piled up with messages. I returned some of them. I told my father I was okay and would go to work soon. I kept in touch with my office. Sara, my aunt and my mother's only sibling, called every day the first week, then once a week.

She told me stories when I was little, when we would sit on the sand in Ocean City. She would talk of Neptune and his armies of the waters, of rivers on the ocean floor, and later of the man who fished for forty days and didn't catch a fish, the man with just a boy to help him with his skiff, the boy who stayed his friend when luck had left. Later I read that story, and her telling lingered in my head, the way she told about the boy.

I didn't call Sara. I remembered the boy in the story. I know it's not meant to be his story. I used to like to think it was, pretending I could choose, the way my mother did when she adopted me.

On the Wednesday one month later, I went outside and commemorated my mother's early death, my loss of her when we were both still young. I stood in front of my apartment in Georgetown on the cobblestone path. I watched dust swirl in sun. I thought about how, when I laid my face against my mother's arm the day she told me I was adopted, I could feel the sun on her skin and smell the sea. Then I went back in the house and called my friend Francisca.

Francisca and I drink together. I've known Francisca for a long time though she and I are very different. Francisca cleans houses. She's a middle-class white woman, thirty-one years old, honey blond hair, long polished fingernails, always manicured. Hands like my mother's. I once asked her how she could clean and still have hands like that. She said her nails were like iron— that it was inherited. Her mother's nails were like that too. They never broke. "In fact," she said, "I use them like tools when I'm cleaning. Maybe I'm not human," she said. "I have claws like a wild thing," and she laughed.

Francisca doesn't laugh much. She lost a baby when she was in her twenties. The baby was three years old when she died from a congenital heart defect. There was nothing Francisca could do. And then there was no way she could recover. She divorced her husband. She started cleaning houses and has a good business now. She still does most of the work herself. She says, "It's like cleaning out the closets in my head, like fixing things." But I know that Francisca will never be fixed.

We went to Morton's, an upscale steak house, a block from my apartment. The maitre d' George flirts with me. He's about fifty-five and thinks I'll probably sleep with him some day. He said, "Sasha, where have you been, my love? Come sit at the bar with me for a few minutes before we get busy."

I'd gotten there early. I wanted to walk in alone. I wanted to sit by myself, get ready for Francisca, ready for talking again. I told George I'd been away. I didn't tell him about my mother. I would tell him eventually but not that night. He brought me a glass of red zinfandel, my favorite, the Jack London. I once bought a bottle for Sara, and she recalled the story by London, a story she'd read to me, the one about building a fire. She didn't appreciate the wine. At Morton's I sat at the bar and thought about the man in the snow, the matches and sticks that wouldn't light. I sipped the wine George handed me, enjoyed the berries on my tongue, the way the wine warmed my throat. And then Francisca arrived.

She'd just showered. I could see moist strands of hair at the nape of her neck. When we kissed hello, I could smell the soap on her skin. Her makeup was heavy around the eyes, too heavy, I thought. That's how I'd done mine, how I'd needed to do it.

We sat together at the bar.

"Rough time, huh, Sash?"

"Um, but at least I'm out."

"I've missed you," she said. "I've needed to talk to you."

I needed her to need me this way. I understood that Francisca was what I needed because she was unlucky.

"How's Richard?" I asked. I knew he had to be the problem. Francisca had met Richard at Morton's. He bought her a big steak and a thirty dollar bottle of red wine to go with it. She thought that showed her something important about him, about his staying power. Francisca is looking for staying power. She thought she'd found it in Richard, but I knew it couldn't last because Francisca has to lose to keep her grief alive.

"I got a detective to follow him," she said.

"Whatever for?"

"Sash, he got soft in bed. Now I realize he's forty, but still that's not supposed to happen. And I told him, of course. I mean

I have enough problems without feeling like the guy can't get it up for me. You understand."

This was classic Francisca. She told me this detective followed Richard to his ex-wife's house, saw them open a bottle of wine in the kitchen, that he stayed all night. That was it for Francisca. She booted Richard out, told him he couldn't commit and she could never trust him.

"You're sure about that?"

"Yeah, he's not worth it."

"I like that about you, your certainty." That's what Francisca's child, that perfect gift she'd lost had given her. "It's your best quality. My mother had that. Your turn."

She laughed. "Your best quality? True blue. You stick."

"Yeah, well, Sara keeps calling and I don't call her back. Weird, huh?"

"Yeah, considering."

Francisca knew I used to go to Sara's house for dinner once a week, every week, that I started having dinner with Sara and her husband Ben and their teenage daughter Rebecca when I started school at Georgetown U. I ate with them at the long wood table in her kitchen in Chevy Chase. I didn't tell my mother about the visits. I didn't go home to Baltimore much. Just occasionally on the weekends or when I had to, when my mother was in the hospital. She was in and out most of my life, most of Sara's life.

That was the year I started drinking, the year I met Francisca.

"Sash, for God's sake, find out how she is."

"I know how she is."

Once, in the hospital, when my mother was on the gurney on her way to another operating room I saw them, no words—just eyes and fingers that made me think of a photo in the album: Sara, a little girl in baggy shorts, white anklets and canvas Keds, sitting on an old glider on the narrow porch of their row house; my mother perched on the railing, wearing a halter top and pedal pushers, her hand reaching for the glider's metal arm. In the hospital's linoleum hallway, I watched their fingers part, saw their hands stilled mid-air when an orderly wheeled my mother down the hall. I remember how I thought that I could hear a glider squeak.

Francisca said, with an edge in her voice, "Yeah, sure, you know. And you're sure, right?"

I filled Francisca's glass. "Yeah, I'm sure like you're sure."

I thought of my mother on the surface of the sea. Before the crutches, before the wheel chair because they turn sand into quick sand, we went to the beach at Ocean City, Maryland, every summer. She swore she could sense the exact times within a day when the moon pulls the sea forward and back. We'd go down from the boardwalk, down to the edge of ocean and shore to watch the tides bulge up on the sand and slide away. When she died, it was like a rip in the surface of the ocean, like a current pulling out to sea, water caught between two sandbars underneath, a trap that, if you're in the ocean, you can't see.

The next day I couldn't go to work. I sat at my desk by the window and took out a long yellow pad. With my head clear of the last night's wine, I started a list of everything I know about myself, when I was little.

Here's what I wrote: I kept my eyes closed for a month when I was born. (My mother said it was because I had an eye infection. Sara said I was waiting to be sure to see my mother. My mother loved when Sara said that.) I have dark green eyes. Like the ocean. (My mother used to say that.) Like leaves in spring. (Sara says that.) Deep, dark brown eyes, amber brown. My mother's eyes. (Sara's are like hers but lighter, yellow-brown in the center.) My white ocean of hair. (What Sara called it. Like a peroxide wish, my mother said. She had dark hair she'd once tried to dye and loved the way my hair changed with light, ran her fingers through it, French braided it while it was wet with sea and salt.) My new Mary Janes, yellow patent leather, that I wore to bed. I didn't talk until I was three, then spoke in full sentences. I'm strong-willed like a bull. (My mother said that. Like her, she said.) A sea goddess who came to earth full blown. (Sara said that. She said I came with my own history.) And then I wrote: insulin syringes on the sink, the smell of alcohol on skin. Oranges and grapefruits. Teaching me to put the needles in their skins. The smell of acid in my nose. Piles of pills beside her bed. The way she yelled. The day she hit me when I drank the last orange juice from the fridge. The way her blood ran hot for fighting. The way her blood ran slow inside her narrowed veins. The pain inside her legs and hands. The pills. My drinking. Dinners at Sara's house.

I was at the bottom of the page. Words trailed down the yellow pad, black ink, off the lines, off center, all over the page. I felt smothered, sucked under, choked.

I longed to talk to Sara, to sit across from her. I could see her in the middle thwart of her safe skiff, her oar lying in the sea, waiting for my hands to wrap around, take hold, be pulled across the side.

I called her.

"Sasha, Sasha." That's what she said when she heard my voice—just my name, again and again, and then she waited.

I asked her to lunch.

We agreed to meet at the Mayflower hotel in the restaurant off the lobby. I wore one of my black suits. I was perfectly put together, understated gold earrings, flat suede Ferragamo shoes, black stockings, swingy but professional black skirt, elegant ivory and black patterned vest with scroll-wrapped tiny buttons, and an Armani tailored jacket. I was sitting in the lobby waiting for her when I glanced down and noticed the smudge on my cuff. Had I inadvertently wiped my nose on my sleeve or, more likely, dragged my cuff across the foamy top of my morning cappuccino?

I was alarmed by my sleeve.

Sara was wearing a black sweater and slacks, oddly casual for her job. She directs one of the research departments at the Library of Congress. I like to think she works in an attic room, a book open on her lap, a window filled with rustling leaves. Quiet work. "Unlike my noisy childhood," she'd said once. "Noisy how?" I'd asked, and after a long pause, the silence before speech that is the sound of sadness, she'd said, "Illness makes a lot of noise." And I sat silent, thinking of my mother's sickness, how it must have filled her house the way it filled up mine.

"I took the day off," she said. I gave her my cheek. She tried to hug me, but quickly stepped back when I pulled away. I stood and looked at her. Sara is three years younger than my mother, tall and thin, prettier in an odd way—strong bones in her face that give her a look of knowing. It's the way the bones dominate in her face, not the flesh, as if I can see her core, her skeleton. I don't have that kind of bone thinness. My mother didn't either. My mother admired Sara's bones and her skin, smooth and fair like their mother's. My mother had skin that tanned and wrinkled. She sat in the sun all summer managing the pool near her house. She couldn't have a job like Sara's or mine. The illness that took over her life when she was twelve and finally took it away when she was forty-six and I was twenty-five marked her territory—the way her death marked mine.

"Yeah, well, I've taken the month off," I told her.

"Yes." That was all she said. Then she waited. That's her way. Not like my mother at all.

"But I'm okay now. I've been back to work for a week. I just needed to be alone, really alone to think."

"I've been worried," she said.

"I got your messages, but I just couldn't talk. I need to be alone," I said again. I wanted to explain why I couldn't let her help me. But how to put in words what I had yet to understand: this pull, this tow?

"Without me?" she asked.

I didn't answer. Instead I looked at her and wondered if *she* went outside when she was little to get away from the noise inside her house, if *she* sat on the curb, if she wished herself away.

We ate. She picked at her salad. A chicken Caesar salad. She'd ordered what I'd ordered as if the food didn't matter to her and then she didn't really eat it. So I guess it didn't. But then I thought, That's why she's so thin. Never eats. My mother used to say that. She'd say, "Sara gets throat lock when she's nervous. Can't get anything down and since she's nervous most of the time, she's thin like a rail." She'd say to Sara, "If only I could get such an ailment." And then my mother and Sara would laugh, a kind of private, morbid joke. My mother, after all, was sick.

I'd made it hard for Sara to eat.

When we left the restaurant, she suggested coffee in the lounge in the lobby. She said, "You could smoke there and we could talk some more."

Sara stopped smoking fifteen years ago when my mother had the first operation on her leg. My mother told Sara she had to stop smoking because she wanted her alongside. And Sara did because my mother had to stop. Sara never started again. I was only ten and couldn't go on the trip. I stayed home with my father who said he had to work, who worked more and more as my mother got more sick, more often. They went to Milwaukee because the veins in my mother's body had all narrowed and even the doctors at Johns Hopkins didn't think they could find new veins to save her leg. But there was this doctor, as my mother said, "in God-awful Milwaukee," who could do it.

We got our cappuccinos and it was as if Sara read my mind as I lit up. "The first thing your mother did after the first operation on her legs was put a cigarette in her mouth. What a pistol she was. She lit it up just the way you're doing now, only she had an IV in her arm and she did it right in front of the doctor. She lit it and when he told her not to smoke, that it would only make things worse, she smiled wide and showed those great teeth of hers and said oh so sweetly, 'Fuck you.' "

I laughed. Sara had never told me that one before.

"Still," she said, "I wish you wouldn't smoke."

"It's one of the advantages of being adopted," I said. "I don't have to worry about heredity."

"How does that make any sense?"

"Because I don't know what it could make worse."

I looked down into the white cup and stirred the foam and cinnamon. I watched the fluid circle round my spoon like a little whirlpool. The cup had a gold rim like the Royal Worcester mug, the one I gave my mother one Mother's Day. She always used it, at least when I was around. She never put it in the dishwasher because of the 14-carat gold rim. She used to warm her hands around the cup, her long red nails, how the polish always glowed. She took such care of her hands, getting manicures once a week. Those perfect nails around the peaches and the grapes on the mug, the purple blue veins in her frigid fingers. I began to weep, right there in the Mayflower coffee bar.

Sara put her hand on top of mine. She didn't say anything. Just put her warm, perfect hand on mine. Her fingers are small and narrow. She keeps her nails trimmed, unpolished. I pulled my hand away.

I remembered the other "Milwaukees" that came one after another—when I was grown like Sara, when I was the one who sat by the bed, when I was too old to find a curb to sit on—when my mother pulled me to her—and when the pull was more than I could bear, how I found another way: with a drink in my hand. I remembered how I laid down a fog inside my head and slept.

Alcohol was the only drug my mother didn't use. She had to kill the pain in ways she understood. That meant prescriptions written out by doctors, purchased in drugstores. She disapproved of drinking. She thought it was low and dirty. It was my drug and she knew it. She knew it because, when I came home, I came home drunk. She waited for me alone, while my father worked his second job, the night job. She never slept even with the drugs. She'd drop off now and then, but the pain in her legs and hands would soon take over. I asserted once, "You use drugs and I use booze and there's not a whole lot of difference—still get a good high," but she didn't agree.

One night I came home and stood at the end of her bed. I reeked from beer and bourbon. I could smell it on my skin, rising out of my pores in sweat. My mother lay dozing in bed, her hair, cut in layers, feathered out on the pillow, her profile defined on the cotton pillow slip. I could see the curve of her nose, the angle of her brow, the parting of her lips. I couldn't believe she was really asleep. I thought she was dead. I walked to the edge of her bed and kneeled down in my rocky, boozy haze. I put my face next to her mouth. I could hear the air inside her lungs. I smelled her breath. It was acrid with smoke and chemicals and loss. She opened her eyes and reached out for me. I thought she was going to hold me, embrace me. She took my long hair into her hands and pulled me screaming on top of her on the bed. She pulled my jaws open and pushed her face into my mouth. She wrenched my head and neck. My back arched. My body shook. I quivered with her anger, lying on her stomach, her breasts pressed against mine. She was strong. She could break me in half.

"What are you doing," she screamed into my open mouth. It was a curse, not a question. "What are you doing to this body that I saved and raised. What right have you. Who do you think you are."

And then the questions: "You think you know pain? You think you hurt? You think you need to numb your mind?"

She threw me on the floor. I reached up to her bedstand and with my heavy, drunken arm swept all the amber, white-capped bottles to the floor. Then I got up and went into my room to sleep it off.

And once a week I went for calm, for respite from the noise of illness. I went to dinner at Sara's house.

After we'd finished our coffee, when I'd pulled myself together, after Sara had paid the check, she said. "Let's go for a walk."

"I'm sorry," I said. "I have to go now. It's been good to see you."

"But Sasha, I've got the whole day. We could go outside and just walk the way we used to."

Once we walked along the tidal basin in early April when the gnarled cherry trees bloom. It was early morning before we both went to work. I was hung over and needed to talk. She met me. She walked alongside me. The morning was cold and it sobered me, reminded me of my mother like an upwelling current from the bottom of the sea.

"No, we can't do that," I said. "We can't."

"Why can't we? We can. Of course we can."

"No." I put my hand up like a signal that she shouldn't come any closer.

"Will you come to dinner then, maybe next week?"

"I'll call you," I said, and then I went for a walk, a long walk but not where Sara and I used to walk. I walked the long down-town blocks, one after another, down L Street, over to K, all the way to Georgetown as fast as I could. The sun was high and hot. I pulled off my suit jacket and slung it over my shoulder, kept walking until I got to my apartment. My ivory silk blouse stuck to my skin. I pulled it off over my head without unbuttoning it, pulled my bra off the same way. Unzipped my skirt, kicked my shoes into the wall, ripped off my panty hose and threw them in the trash. I got in the shower and let the water run down my body. Then I lay down on the floor in the shower stall, curled up, wedged into the square of tile. I smelled water, soap, and mold. I cried. Tears and water in the drain.

I longed for the force of will that would give my life a seam-
less, silent glide through space and time. I longed for my
mother's will.

My mother lost a baby before she adopted me. Sara was sixteen
when my mother lost the baby. She said that one day about a
year after the baby had died she went to the movies at the Crest
theater across from the diner on Rogers Avenue with two girl-
friends to see *The Young Doctors* starring Ben Gazzara. She told me
how the white light flickered off the screen like Ben Gazzara's
white coat, like all the white coats rushing past her when her face
was pressed against the nursery glass. How he delivered a baby.
How he placed the crying child in the mother's arms. Sara told
me she began to cry, that she wept uncontrollably, unable to
explain. How her chocolate-covered raisins rolled on the floor.
She said she remembered it as a moment of excess that lingered
inside her, disturbed her and slowly developed like a strip of film
in solution in a darkroom. I didn't understand then what she
meant, but the memory has slowly revealed itself, made me see
how much my mother lost before she found me.

When she was pregnant she went to the hospital more than
two months before her due date to ensure a safe delivery. My
mother told me the doctor put her in a section of the hospital for
the terminally ill. She said he did that because the patients there
were allowed to walk outside or ride in wheelchairs to a garden,
and visitors weren't limited by special hours. But my mother
wasn't terminally ill, or that's what people thought in those days
about her disease. Like me they didn't understand how sick she
was, how she would die, that she would die young. In this special
place my mother waited for her baby to grow and form. The
doctor said he was taking the baby early because he feared an
oversized baby, hard to deliver. He said diabetics have such

babies. But he took it too early. As my mother lay recuperating from the Cesarean section, the doctor told her that her baby's lungs hadn't fully formed. My mother told me she watched the baby's chest heave up and down behind the nursery glass and that the baby died after twenty-three hours.

Since my mother had a disease, it was hard for her to get a baby from an adoption agency. It was possible but hard, and my mother wasn't good at waiting. She found a doctor, an obstetrician who told her there were other ways to get babies. And with his help, she got me. A woman handed me over in a hospital. I know because my mother told me. A woman gave me like a gift. That's what I think on a good day. Or like returned merchandise, on a bad day.

On the Wednesday night one week later, I took with me to Morton's the little ceramic box edged in silver that Sara had given me one birthday. It was hand painted with a soft, gray-green design. It was quite elegant. In the note, she'd said, "This little box reminds me of the undersides of new blown leaves like the color of your eyes."

I gave it to Francisca after we finished a bottle of the Jack London Zinfandel. I told Francisca that the box reminded me of the child she lost, though I had never seen her.

"It's small and light in the hand," I said, "like a memory."

Francisca wept, remembering.

I ordered another bottle of wine for the two of us. George, the maitre d', brought it over himself. "For you, my love," he said, "I'll pour."

"It's Wednesday," I said. "Let's drink to my mother. Let's drink to motherhood."

I waited two weeks to call Sara. I called and asked if I could come to dinner. She said, "Any night you want." I said I wanted a night when Ben was working late so we could be alone. I knew Rebecca was away at school, Wesleyan in Connecticut.

When I went away—though not far enough away at Georgetown—Sara, living in Washington, made it convenient for me to stop in and I did it more than I thought I would, told myself it had just worked out that way. Now I understand I went to Sara's house instead of going home.

I would come early and help her cook. We were often alone in the kitchen fixing dinner for the others.

Copper pots hung from the ceiling over the stove, tarnished, scratched. She has a rough, tin Foley grinder up there on the rack. She uses it for mashed potatoes. She hangs strainers and ladles and a stock pot from the hooks.

She showed me how to season the old cast iron frying pan we used for hot peppered fish. She never washes it. Just pours boiling water on it and then wipes it down with oil and hangs it up again. I loved the hot peppered fish. Sometimes I would stop on my way and buy the halibut. When I got to her house, she would be in the kitchen, pounding the pepper for the coating on the fish, heating the frying pan until it smoked. I would take the fish out of the ice and butcher paper and roll it in the crushed pepper on the long waxed paper on the counter. I would lay the fish in the smoking pan while she chopped cilantro for the garnish. I remember the bottle of extra virgin olive oil in her hand, its clear green color in the bottle, the way it glistened when she drizzled it across the blackened fish. I remember the smell of burnt pepper and cast iron.

It was a Tuesday night when I arrived at Sara's door again. I'd brought nothing. No offering, no flowers, no wine. She didn't seem to notice. She was wearing the blue faded apron she always used to wear when she opened the door. She had the long white strings tied around her narrow middle so the knot came out in the front, just below her hip. The front was smudged with flour.

Her face was bare, no makeup at all. She was always careful with her makeup. Never wore very much but made sure that the bare truth of her age was covered. That night I could see the lines around her eyes, the shadows underneath.

We went into the kitchen. She poured peanut oil into a big pot. A pile of raw, sliced potatoes floated in a large pot of cold water on the counter near the stove. "French fries," she said. And then she looked at me. Remember, her eyes said.

And I did.

"Suntan lotion and French fries, my favorite smells," my mother used to say. My mother loved the honky-tonk of the lower end of the boardwalk. She loved the crowd, the noise, the dark, greasy air. She was the French fry expert and would buy them only from Thrasher's where they fried them in their skins in vats of peanut oil. The fries filled up in great big paper cones. She poured salt and vinegar on top. Then we went to Dumser's Dairy for a custard ice cream cone. We always had vanilla. She used to lick mine around the edges, catching the melting sweetness while I ate from the top. And then we'd ride the Ferris wheel. With our stomachs full, we'd take the slow slide around the sky. My mother loved the swaying stillness at the top when the wheel stopped turning to let the others off at the bottom. She used to say, "I hope we get stuck up here. It happens sometimes. It happened to me and Sara once. Maybe we'll be lucky like that."

Sara lowered French fries into the oil with a large slotted spoon. I said, "You still went, didn't you?"

"To the beach? Well, sure. We took Rebecca. But it was never the same, Sasha."

While we rocked up there on the Ferris wheel, alone together, my mother always put her arm across my shoulder and held me. I could see kites flying on the beach in reflected light from the boardwalk. I could hear the waves in the sea in the quiet of that waiting, airy moment. I could smell the sun on my mother's skin.

Sara stirred the fries with the spoon. I could smell the peanut oil. And then she said, "You went too with your friends when you got older."

"Oh sure, we drank and caroused. On the loose, you might say."

"Wild, like your mother."

"Like my mother," I said, "right." At the end of the boardwalk in Ocean City, the sand stretches out so far, it's hard to see the ocean. My mother is that place. She's the end of the boardwalk where the old wooden boards stop and the cement walk begins, where the food and the rides are, where the honky-tonk begins, where the Ferris wheel takes its slide around the sky.

Now Sara pressed freshly ground pepper into the tops of hamburgers and sautéed them on a bed of hot salt in a sizzling frying pan. She added lemon juice and Worcestershire sauce to the pan when the burgers were browned. She put a piece of butter on the top of each burger and I watched it melt. I watched her make a salad. I watched her chop garlic and put it in a wooden bowl. I watched her pour in balsamic vinegar and Dijon mustard. I watched her use a whisk to swirl in olive oil for the dressing. I watched her do all the things my mother never did.

At the long wood table in her kitchen, I sat down and she poured me a glass of wine. I drank from her green crystal glass with the clear white, delicate stem and said, "I came here too often, when I should have gone home."

She said, "Your mother was very sick, Sasha, for a long time, for most of the time."

"And I'm my mother's child," I said. It was the only way I could explain. It is the explanation, the only explanation.

After dinner, I didn't help her with the dishes the way I used to. I didn't carry one single plate to the sink. I sat and drank my wine and watched her wash the dishes, scour the pan, pour the used oil into old coffee cans she'd saved under the sink. I didn't help her lift the heavy pot. I watched perspiration form at the edge of her white upper lip. I watched her move and walk in her big, wide kitchen. I looked for my mother in the angle of her back. But they're so different. I could see the tiny bones in the back of her neck. It was like looking through her skin. I thought of my mother in a shroud beneath the ground.

When it was time for me to go, I stood at Sara's open door and looked out into the night. She was at my side and I could smell her skin. It was not the smell of my mother's skin. I could smell her breath, fragrant with wine and garlic. It was not the smell of my mother's breath.

"I'm my mother's child," I said again and thought how I'd always known that I was all she had.

The tide rises to its apogee in answer to the moon and sun and earth when they align. A rip defies this call. My mother used to say, "If you get caught, you need to know the trick of swimming parallel to shore—the best way to get out. Or just let go." She meant just float and you'll get out.

Sara turned me toward her with her arms on my shoulders. She grabbed me and pulled me to her chest. I could feel her fine, thin hands against my back.

"Her only child," I said.

"Yes," she said, "you are."

And now I moved away, light and free inside the tow. However far it goes.

The Woman Who Never Cooked

There once was a woman with three hundred and twenty-seven cookbooks who never cooked. She had been a very good cook, accomplished. She could bake a soufflé that would not fall, that rose like a beautiful velvet crown above the edge of her Royal Worcester bowl. She could roll out pastry thin as rice paper for dumplings, sear a steak, revolving it a quarter turn to make a cross-hatch pattern with charcoaled lines of fire that rose from her gas burner to the cast-iron bottom of her ridged griddle. She could touch the meat's surface with the tip of her finger and know what was in its center: rare, bloody juices or medium pink flesh.

But she cooked no more for reasons that escaped her.

When she was hungry, she ate cheese and crackers from her refrigerator, bought Chinese take-out—always the same dish, "Number 12 Mala String Beans." She went with her husband to restaurants with blackboards outside or in the waiting areas, where she could see the specials, where she could choose from a short list before sitting down because menus, all the choices, like all the recipes she'd memorized, disturbed her.

She would stand in front of her cookbooks and study them, as if their titles would yield up the answer to her dilemma, the dilemma of the one who has survived: what does she deserve?

The cookbooks stood on the longest and widest shelf of her library, where she kept her favorite family pictures displayed on the shelf in the middle, where she kept the brass mortar and pestle and the two candlesticks that had come on the boat from Latvia in the one valise her grandmother had carried when she traveled alone, sent away by her parents to escape the pogrom they knew was coming.

In her library she had one section for Aristotle, Buber, Kant and Nieztsche, the Torah and the Talmud. She remembers in the Talmud the story of two men who are in the desert. Only one of them has water. If the one who has the water shares it, both will die. If he drinks all the water, one will live. She remembers the question: what should he do?

She kept all her poetry together: Auden, Eliot, Stevens, Kunitz, Bishop, Rich, Kinnell, Dickinson, Lawrence. Thick volumes of collected poems with paper clips along the edges of the pages to mark the poems she "needed"—that was the word she used in her head because the words filled her up like food. (Kunitz's pears, the orange on his father's forehead; Bishop's mother's watch—lost. Auden's "time" that says nothing but I told you so.) She had eighty-nine volumes of poetry. She knew because she had counted them the same day she had counted all her cookbooks, around the time she realized she would cook no more.

One day, she thought, I have one cookbook for nearly every day of the year. Though she had known the number of cookbooks for some time, this was a revelation that caused her to stand in front of the cookbooks every night, hoping a single title would reveal the answer. The books were not arranged alphabetically or by type because she was organized but not compulsive and rather enjoyed the disarray of cookbooks and literature and philosophy on her shelves that she'd painted red inside with all the edges and trim beige so that the books covered most of the red, though she could see it, and could enjoy the way the red picked up the deep, swirling colors in her Persian rug.

Books, sectioned off but juxtaposed in odd, thrilling ways.

She believed she learned in a mixed up, sudden way—not in historical periods the way courses in schools are taught—but by the nearness of thoughts laid down in her head. She would look out her window across from the bookcase, close and open her eyes—and in that passing moment, in the shifting light—see trees like black lines on a blank-paper winter sky. This was how she realized, opening paper-clipped pages at random, that Emily Dickinson ("'Tis good—the looking back on Grief—") and D.H. Lawrence ("It is only immoral/ to be dead-alive") were not as different as she once thought.

And so it made sense to her to stand each day in front of the titles of her cookbooks, though *these books* she could no longer open.

In front of *The Silver Palate Cookbook*, she recalled the French toast she made with challah, cream and Grand Marnier, orange peel and cinnamon. She made the challah from her mother's recipe, in the green four-by-six-inch index-card file box, where her mother sometimes placed a recipe according to the name of the sister or niece or cousin who wrote it down for her. She found "challah" under *S* for Sonya, who'd been saved when they hid in a sewer to escape a pogrom. When Sonya cried, when the guide said she must be killed or all would die, she'd suckled at her mother's breast. This challah the woman had learned to make, added honey to the recipe to make it hers, and saw her mother nod and smile when her tongue touched the soft egg bread.

In front of Jacques Pepin's *Art of Cooking*, Volume 2, she remembered the buckwheat blinis she made on New Year's Eve and served to her husband and children with Russian Sevruga caviar. She could not afford Beluga, which was better. Although caviar was kosher, her parents and her grandparents had never had it because, though cheap in Latvia, it was not cheap enough. She remembered how she and her husband and children laughed from the bubbles in the champagne, how they learned to put crème fraîche on the blinis, how she bought a tiny horn spoon to scoop the caviar onto the delicate pancakes. Her children are grown now; one lives in Manhattan, the other in Seattle.

In front of Julia Child's *The Art of French Cooking*, the book Julia coauthored with Simone Beck (she thinks of Julia Child in this familiar way because she learned to cook from taping and watching all her shows), she thought about the paté she made with cognac and butter and swirled into a fine mousse in her Cuisinart, the paté—so different from her mother's that she'd never learned to make though her mother made it every year on Rosh Hashanah and Passover, chopping coarsely the chicken livers sautéed in chicken fat, the hard-boiled egg, the crisp fried onions in a wooden bowl that she now owned because her father gave it to her after her mother's stroke, when her mother's left hand and leg were paralyzed, when her mother could no longer speak in sentences, when she could no longer cook, but before her mother refused to eat, before she said these words "Yitgadal v'yitkadash," the first two words of the mourner's kaddish, the week before she died.

In front of *The Ramognolis' Table*, she remembered the first time she made a béchamel sauce for lasagna. This cream sauce becomes a layer of softness on the palate. It is an essential ingredient that no one she has ever known uses. It lies atop the beef and slowly simmered tomato sauce under the large noodles she used to roll out using her hand cranked pasta machine. This dish she made for her sister's surprise fortieth birthday party, thirteen years before her sister died, after the three heart attacks but before the laser surgery on her eyes, before the blindness, before the amputation.

In front of Martha Stewart's *Pies and Tarts*, she remembered the buttermilk pie she made for her mother and father one Thanksgiving. She used her food processor to make the crust, placing in the processor bowl the flour she kept in the freezer, the tiny pieces of cold butter she cut up with her cool hands, the salt, a pinch of sugar, swirling the ingredients for barely thirty seconds, pouring the ice water through the tube at the top. She rolled out the pastry on the marble board she kept in the refrigerator and she lined the edges of the pie with tiny leaves of pastry she cut out and shaped with a paring knife. Her parents were surprised by the sweetness of the pie and the fine, crisp crust. When she was a child, her father liked to drink buttermilk before he went to bed. She had no taste for sour milk. But she remembered his milky smile before the Parkinson's disease made his face into a mask with a downturned mouth like the buttermilk face she must have made when she first drank it. His face now, a frozen face that showed her how he'd look in death. But he was not dead. He and she were left.

After nearly three hundred days of reading titles, she was drawn solely to desserts, to *Chez Panisse Desserts, Maida Heatter's Book of Great Desserts, Gourmet's Best Desserts, Silver Palate Desserts,* and twenty-three others. Could she do it? Make dessert? The orange cake her mother made every year on her childhood birthdays? But one birthday her mother made the Wellesley fudge cake by mistake. This was her sister's favorite, a bittersweet chocolate cake the woman hated as a child but now had a taste for. Maybe this cake she could make, understanding her mother's mix-up, the blending of her children's favorites, interchangeable desserts, like the woman's grief for her mother, for her sister, for her father who was about to die. But she couldn't remember the recipes for these desserts, though she had known them all by heart, by the rhythm of her hands mixing flour, sugar, butter, eggs—beating them into ribbons of yellow batter. Yellow. Like the lemon meringue pie, the dessert she'd thought was her father's favorite.

But she knew she couldn't make Martha Stewart's recipe for mile-high lemon meringue pie with the twelve egg whites atop the filling that would not set no matter how long she stirred the yellow lemon and butter and sugar mixture on the stove, no matter how long she kept the mixture in the refrigerator to cool, congeal, coalesce. Something must have been missing from the recipe. She made this pie three times: for Thanksgiving, for Father's Day, for her father's birthday. Her mother and father and sister had laughed—and so had she—when she cut into the beautiful pie with its perfect meringue, the pie that sat on her glass pedestal, when they watched the filling run down the glass plate, around the rim, wind its sweet yellow ribbon onto the pedestal, onto the base, onto the fine linen cloth she had laid on the table. The last time she made the pie, while she was laughing, she shouted, "I'll never make your favorite dessert, Daddy. I give up." "But my favorite," he said, "is cherry." She had mixed this up the way her mother mixed up the orange cake and the Wellesley fudge, the way, when her father died, they would all mix up. Deaths piled up before her, memories merged. No way to see them clearly, to figure out the way to grieve. She stood long past the time for dinner in front of all the dessert books that she could no longer open. She could not remember the recipe for a single dessert. She heard inside her head that one repeated word, *desserts*. She stared so hard one *S* inside the titles on the binders dropped away.

She saw just *deserts*—spelled like the place where the two men in the Talmudic question stood.

What did she deserve? There she stood with her father—her mother and her sister, gone. She believed that she had all the water. Would she drink it?

No, she thought, because suddenly she knew what was missing from the recipe, from the yellow ribbon of lemon that would not congeal. She knew that the water must go in the pie, mixed first with a bit of cornstarch for the sweetness to hold firm. She did not know what she deserved or what was just. She knew only that she would make the pie, that it would be hard to make and that it would be her favorite.